D0194704

The 100-Year-Old Secret

by

TRACY BARRETT

Henry Holt and Company
New York

Henry Holt and Company, LLC
Publishers since 1866
175 Fifth Avenue
New York, New York 10010
www.HenryHoltKids.com

Distributed in Canada by H. B. Fenn and Company Ltd.

Library of Congress Cataloging-in-Publication Data
Barrett, Tracy.
The hundred-year-old secret / by Tracy Barrett.—1st ed.
p.   cm. — (The Sherlock files)
Summary: Xena and Xander Holmes, an American brother and
sister living in London for a year, discover that Sherlock Holmes was
their great-great-great-grandfather when they are inducted into the
Society for the Preservation of Famous Detectives and given his
unsolved casebook, from which they attempt to solve the case of a
famous missing painting.
ISBN-13: 978-0-8050-8340-8 / ISBN-10: 0-8050-8340-5
[1. Brothers and sisters—Fiction. 2. England—Fiction. 3. Mystery and
detective stories.] I. Title.
PZ7.B275355Hu 2008
[Fic]—dc22

2007034004

First Edition—2008
Book designed by Greg Wozney
Printed in the United States of America on acid-free paper. ∞

10 9 8 7 6 5 4 3 2 1

CHAPTER 1

If they hadn't been playing the Game that day, if the ballet dancer hadn't happened to walk by, if Xander's dimples and big dark blue eyes hadn't been so appealing, and especially if Xena had waited only five minutes before reading the mysterious note, perhaps none of it would have happened. But it did happen.

To anyone watching Xena and Xander Holmes it might seem like an ordinary Friday afternoon—a sister and her younger brother passing time on the steps of the Dulcey Hotel in London. But to twelve-year-old Xena the day was anything but ordinary. For one thing, they were Americans who had arrived in England only the week before with their parents. For another, the whole family was sharing two very small hotel rooms until they found an apartment. Not to mention that she and Xander had to start at a new school on Monday.

No, the only thing normal was that Xena and Xander were playing the Game. The rules were simple. Whoever guessed something correctly about a passerby—like his job or where he was from—got a point. Today they had a good lookout spot on the front steps with a box of what the doorman called "biscuits." They'd been confused about why they would want to eat biscuits in the middle of the day, but their mother had explained that cookies were called biscuits in England.

Xander noticed a couple strolling past, the man consulting a map while the woman clung to his arm, extending her left hand to admire the gold band on the fourth finger. "Tourists," he said, and then added, "honeymooners."

"Duh," Xena answered. "I wasn't even going to do them. They're too easy. How about him?" She pointed.

Xander took the binoculars and peered at the tired-looking man standing on the corner, waiting for the light to change. Xander shrugged and looked at his sister.

"Gardener," she said. She always enjoyed this part. "Muddy boots." But she knew this wasn't enough. Anybody can have muddy boots, especially in a damp city like London. "Calloused hands. Sunburn on the back of his neck as if he works bent over a lot."

"There's not enough sun here for anyone to get burned," Xander objected.

Xena tried not to think about that. Even in London the sun had to come out *some*time. They would be living there for a whole year and if it was going to be gray and cold every day, well, Xena would rebel and convince her parents that they had to go home to the States. She didn't care if their father had a great job teaching music and composing here. She didn't care if their grandparents had been Londoners. It wasn't fair to make her and Xander come all the way across the ocean if they were going to be cold and damp all the time—especially since they had to leave all their friends back home in sunny Florida.

The man put down his bag, and it gaped open at the top. Xander trained the binoculars on the opening. A trowel and one of those little rake things were poking out. "Darn!" he said. He handed the binoculars back to his sister.

He perked up as a slender girl neared them. Her brown hair was in a neat ponytail, and she moved gracefully. He leaned forward. Aha! "Ballet dancer!" he cried.

"How can you tell?" Xena asked. "A lot of

girls in my martial arts classes and on the track team move like that. Maybe she's an athlete, not a dancer." Xander said nothing, but he had a smug look on his face. Xena squinted at the girl. Nothing. She looked like an ordinary teenager going to meet her friends. "No way," Xena said.

"Way," Xander answered. He hopped off his perch and trotted along next to the girl. She slowed and then stopped.

That's the way it always was. Xander was ten years old and killer cute. Nobody could resist those dimples, that smile, those enormous eyes. Even the blond streak in his brown curls seemed charming on a boy, whereas Xena thought the same streak looked freaky on her.

The girl laughed at something Xander said and then dug a card out of the bag slung over her shoulder. She gave it to him, tousled his hair in a way that Xena knew he found annoying, and then waved at him as he bounded back up the stairs.

"What is that?" she asked, and he tossed the card in her lap. MISS ROSE'S SCHOOL OF DANCE, she read. CLASSES, PRIVATE LESSONS, CONSULTATIONS. And then an address and phone number.

"I told her I was interested in ballet and asked her where I could get lessons," he said, not even trying to hide the smugness in his voice.

"Okay," she said, "how did you know?"

"Easy." He took a bite of his cookie. "The way her feet pointed out when she walked—you know, not pigeon-toed, the other one."

Xena groaned. She hadn't picked up on that.

"That's how dancers walk. And her bag," he went on. "It had a picture of those shoes on it, the ones they dance in. And—"

"Okay, okay," Xena said. He didn't need to rub it in.

It used to be that she *always* won the Game. Her father had taught it to her when she was in second grade. He would pick her up from school, and as they sat in the car waiting for Xander to finish his Pee Wee Soccer practice, he'd show her how to look for clues.

Xena had been great at the Game from the beginning, sometimes even beating her dad. He'd love it when she'd get one right and would brag about it to her mom.

Then Xander learned how to do it too. Dad had been so proud the day a man in a blue uniform walked by, putting letters into mailboxes, and Xander had yelled, "Mailman!" Dad had cheered as though Xander had done something really amazing. Once when some kids overheard Xena and Xander playing the Game and called them weird, their dad told them that Grandpa had taught it to him, and that Grandpa had learned it from his own dad, so it was a family legacy and something to be proud of.

But now Xander was starting to catch up with Xena. She was furious with herself for missing the ballet shoes stenciled on the girl's dance bag. How obvious can you get?

So when a man came hurrying down the steps next to them and pressed a piece of paper in her hand, she was preoccupied and didn't even think to look at him or call after him or anything. When she heard him mutter "It fades fast," she looked up, startled. She got an impression of someone short and round, with white hair sticking up on the top of his head, and then he was gone.

"What's that?" Xander tried to snatch the paper from her hand, but she held it out of his reach until he settled down. Then she opened it and started reading. Xander leaned against her shoulder, breathing cookie breath into her face.

My dears, the paper read. *My very, very dears. I speak for the whole Society for the Preservation of Famous Detectives (SPFD) when I say that we are thrilled beyond words to welcome you to England, the home of your ancestors.*

Xena stopped reading. She exchanged a puzzled glance with Xander, then turned her eyes back to the paper.

Please allow the SPFD to welcome you more formally. Go to The Dancing Men (if you're hungry, they make an excellent ploughman's lunch) and ask for a saucer of milk for your snake. Then all will be revealed.

"The ink's fading!" Xander exclaimed. Xena read the last few words hurriedly.

Please do not delay. We long to make you welcome. Time, as your illustrious ancestor used to say, is of the essence.
Sincerely,

The pale blue ink disappeared before she could read the signature.

"What does it mean?" Xander asked.

Xena shook her head. She had no clue.

But they were about to find out.

CHAPTER 2

Xena refolded the paper and stared at it. "What's with this disappearing ink?" she asked.

"I thought that was something made up in spy movies," Xander said.

"And what does this mean, milk for our snake?" Xena wondered aloud. "We don't even have a snake."

"Snakes don't drink milk anyway," Xander said. He screwed up his face, his eyes closed, and Xena could tell that he was putting his photographic memory to work. In another minute he spoke as though reading from an encyclopedia, which, in a way, he was.

"Most snakes are carnivores," he recited, "or insectivores." He paused, and Xena knew that he was mentally skimming the next few paragraphs. He opened his eyes. "Nope," he said. "No milk."

"And I don't think they drink out of saucers," she said. "Do they?"

He scrunched up his face again. Then he opened his eyes and shrugged. "No mention of saucers. It's got to be some kind of code . . . or a *password*," he said, his eyes growing even larger with excitement.

"Who was that guy?" she asked. "Did you get a good look at him?"

Xander shook his head. "Nope," he said. "I wasn't paying attention. Why would he want us to go see some dancing men? And what did he mean about our illustrious ancestor?"

"Well, *illustrious* means 'famous,' right? So maybe he thinks we're related to the famous detective Sherlock Holmes," Xena said with a laugh.

"I wish," Xander said. He loved reading mysteries, especially the ones about Sherlock Holmes because they shared the same last name. Plus they were great stories.

"The note sounded as if the person who wrote it knows us," Xena added. "How did it start, again?"

"My dears. My very, very dears," Xander recited.

"And what's a plooman's lunch?" Xena asked, pronouncing the first syllable of *plough-man* as if it rhymed with *through*.

"I think it's a pluffman's lunch," he answered, rhyming the first syllable with *rough*.

"Actually, it's pronounced *plowman*," said a voice behind them. Xena and her brother turned. It was the doorman, the friendly one who had given them the cookies.

"So what's a plowman's lunch?" Xena asked.

"Oh, it's a nice piece of bread and some cheese and pickle. Standard pub fare." He smacked his lips. "They do a good one at The Dancing Men."

"The Dancing Men?" Xander asked. "But that's—"

Xena dug her elbow into his ribs to keep him from saying anything about the letter. After all, there was nothing left to read, and the doorman would think that they were nutty Americans if they showed him a blank piece of paper. Xander poked her back with his own pointy elbow.

"The pub over there," the doorman said, leaning forward and pointing down the street. "They'll fix you right up. It's about lunchtime now, isn't it?"

Xena and Xander looked at each other. "Well," Xander said, "Mom did give us money for lunch. All she said was that we had to be at the hotel by the time she got back from her meeting with the real estate lady."

"Mom thinks we're going to eat at McDonald's," Xena objected. "And, anyway, a pub is a kind of a bar, isn't it? Can we even get in?"

They turned to the doorman, who nodded. "Oh, sure you can. Just don't order a drink, not even a shandy!" He laughed.

"Let's go, Xena!" Xander was hopping from one foot to the other.

Xena considered. What could be wrong with going? Their mother hadn't said anything specific about McDonald's, after all. "Okay," she said. "Come on!" She was as curious about the note as Xander was.

"I thought we'd understand everyone in England because they speak the same language," Xander said as they pushed open the door to the pub with the dancing stick figures on the sign above it. "But *English* English is confusing. They spell *plow* differently and they call cookies biscuits and they drink something called a shandy . . ."

The pub seemed like a cross between a bar and a restaurant. There were small wooden tables all over, and a lot of people stood or sat at the bar, eating lunch. The ones who weren't talking were watching soccer on the large TV. A rushed-looking waitress waved them to a table, and when she had a chance to come over to them, she seemed pleased that they knew already what they wanted.

"You'll like that," she said. "It's my own kids' favorite."

After she had taken a bite, Xena said, "Yum! And it costs even less than what Mom gave us for McDonald's."

"I'll have a shandy," Xander said when the waitress came back to check on them.

The waitress laughed. "I'll bring you one without the beer in it," she said. A few minutes later she returned with two glasses of lemon soda, which she called "lemonade."

"So a shandy is a mixture of lemon soda and beer?" Xena asked, wrinkling her nose. "Yuck."

She took a sip of her soda. "So what do you think this society thing is?" she asked.

"The Society for the Preservation of Famous Detectives," Xander said.

"I know that's their name," said Xena. "But I mean, I wonder what they do. And why did they ask us to come here?"

"Maybe it's some publicity stunt," he said. "The Society gives those mysterious notes to random people and when the ink disappears they get curious and come see what it's about."

Xena looked around at the bustling room. "I don't think this place needs publicity," she said.

Xander shrugged and finished his lemonade. "So what about the snake thing? Shouldn't we ask for the milk for our snake?"

"I don't know." Xena was reluctant. "Don't you think that's some kind of a joke? I don't want the waitress to think we're crazy."

"Oh, come on," Xander urged her. "Let's take a chance. If she thinks we're nuts, we don't have to come back."

They were finishing up when the waitress came by and asked if they wanted anything else. They hesitated and glanced at each other.

Xena took a deep breath. "Just some milk," she said.

"A glass of milk, coming right up," the waitress said, and she started to walk away.

"No," Xander piped up. "Not a glass of milk. A *saucer*."

The waitress froze.

"For our snake," Xena said, and held her breath.

The waitress turned back to them, and the expression on her face was hard to read. Was it confused? Excited? Before Xena could decide, the waitress nodded and put down her order pad. "Follow me," she said. "It's in the back here." She started off at a brisk walk toward the rear of the pub.

Now it was Xena's turn to freeze. She didn't know what she was expecting, but it certainly wasn't this. "Maybe we shouldn't—" she started, but Xander hopped up and darted after the waitress.

"Wait!" Xena called after him. He either didn't hear her or was ignoring her, so she pushed back her chair and flew after the two figures as they disappeared through a curtain at the back of the room. By the time she caught up with them they were at the end of a long bare corridor.

"In there," the woman was saying as she pointed at a dark brown wooden door with a gleaming metal knob.

Before Xena could stop him, Xander opened it and stepped into a dimly lit room.

Xena leaped in after him and grabbed his wrist. "What are you doing?" she demanded. "Following a stranger like that? Mom is going to *kill*—"

But before she had the chance to finish her sentence, the door slammed shut, the thud followed by an ominous click. Xena tried the knob but knew even before it refused to turn that it was no use. That click told her what she didn't want to know. She rattled the knob. Nothing.

The door was locked. They were trapped.

CHAPTER 3

What's the matter?" Xander asked. Why was Xena messing with the door when they could be trying to find out what that snake message meant?

Xena didn't answer right away. Her long brown hair hung over her face, hiding her expression. She *knew* they shouldn't have come in here. "The door is locked," she said.

"Let me try," Xander said, pushing her aside.

The knob turned smoothly, and the door moved a fraction of an inch when he yanked on it. But then it stopped.

"Yup. It's locked." He fought back a surge of fear and turned to take in their surroundings.

"What is this, a storeroom?" he asked. It was filled with boxes in uneven piles on a concrete floor. Dust swirled in the weak afternoon sunlight slanting down from the only window, set high on one wall.

Xena didn't answer, but instead said, trying

to sound calm, "I'm sure the waitress didn't mean to lock us in. I'm sure she's on her way back to let us out."

Xander sneezed.

"Bless you," Xena said automatically.

Xander turned back to the door and pounded on it. "Help!" he shouted. No answer, so he kicked it. "Ow!" He hopped on his other foot and sneezed again.

"It's no use," Xena said. "That hallway we came through was deserted. No one will hear you unless they happen to be standing right outside the door. We'll just have to find another way out, that's all." They both gazed up at the window.

Xander pulled one of the big boxes over to the wall and started to climb on it, but the cardboard collapsed under his foot. He tried another one, hoping it was stronger. Still no good. Time for Xena to do her thing.

"Can you get to it?" Xander asked, looking at the window. Aside from being an excellent long-distance runner and having a black belt in karate, Xena was an expert rock climber.

Xena nodded. "Piece of cake." She took off her running shoes and her socks, spat on her hands, rubbed them together, and started pulling herself up the cinder-block wall.

Compared with some of the rock walls she had scaled back home, this was as simple as climbing a ladder. The cinder-block surface was irregular, and her toes and fingers found easy purchase as her long arms and legs moved smoothly, pulling her toward the light. Most people said she climbed like a cat, but Xander thought she looked more like a spider.

In next to no time she was high above him, her hands gripping the windowsill. She peered out through the dirty glass.

"Go on!" Xander called. "What are you waiting for? Call for help! Climb out and get someone!"

Xena looked down at him over one shoulder. "There's no one out there," she said, and the defeated tone of her voice made his heart sink. "It's an alley or something. And there are bars on the window. Even if I broke the glass I couldn't get out."

She descended more slowly than she had gone up and then dropped the last few feet, landing lightly on her toes. She put her socks and shoes back on and glanced at her brother. He looked so worried that she swallowed her own fear.

"Don't worry," she said. "We'll get out of here. I promise." Fortunately he didn't ask her how. Now if she could only reassure herself as well as her little brother. "Okay, let's figure this out," she said. "Where are we, anyway?"

Both of them looked around again. "Some kind of storeroom," Xander said. He inspected one of the boxes. "'Tableware—Seconds,'" he read. "What does that mean?"

"You know," Xena said. "Remember those sheets that Mom got where the colors didn't match? Those were seconds. They're cheaper than the first-quality ones. They must buy a lot of things like that for the pub."

"Well, that's not going to help much." Xander kicked a box labeled DISHES—DEFECTIVE, and the box flopped onto its side.

"That's weird," Xena commented. "The box is sealed but it seems empty." She dropped to her knees and pried it open. They both looked inside.

"It *is* empty," Xander said.

"I guess they already took the dishes out," Xena said.

"But why would they leave the empty box taped shut in here?" Xander said. He noticed a large carton, about waist high, marked BAKERS— IRREGULAR. It was against a wall next to another one that read LINEN—SECONDS. He gave the linens box a shove, and it slid easily across the floor.

"You know, those first two boxes broke when I tried to stand on them," he said. "They must have been empty too. But all these empty boxes are taped and piled up, as if someone's going to use them. I wonder why."

"It's like they're props in a play or something," Xena said slowly, "or else someone wants this to look like a storeroom, but it isn't." So what was it?

And something was different about the box labeled BAKERS—IRREGULAR, but what? It was dented and dusty and there were holes on the top, though most of the other boxes weren't in great shape either, so that wasn't it. Xander ran his hand along the top of the box, and then realized something. "Xena," he said.

"Hmmm?" Xena replied. She was staring up at the window, trying to figure out a way to break through the bars. She knew she was strong, but not *that* strong.

"Look at this." He pointed to the top of the weird box. "This dust. It isn't real."

"What do you mean, the dust isn't real? How can it be fake dust?"

"I don't know," Xander said. "But I think it's

glued on, or painted on. It doesn't come off." He swept his hand over the top of the carton again. "See? No dust. And no sneeze."

Xena got up and crossed to the box. "Now, that's weird," she said. "Why would someone want to make something look dusty?"

Xander tapped on the box. Something about the phrase *Bakers—Irregular* seemed familiar, but when he tried to remember where he had seen— or heard—the words before, it slipped away from him. He closed his eyes in concentration, shutting out all sound except his own breathing.

Xena knew better than to interrupt him when he was thinking, but she was getting more and more anxious. If this had all been a mistake, the waitress would have come back by now. What was going on? Who wanted them locked up in here? And how would they get out?

"Got it!" Xander's voice broke in on her thoughts. "The Baker Street Irregulars!"

Xena shook her head in bewilderment.

"In my Sherlock Holmes book," he added.

"I never read it, remember?" Xena said. "So what did it say?"

"Well, there were these kids. Sherlock Holmes hired them to be like a detective squad for him. Sherlock lived on Baker Street, so he called them the Baker Street Irregulars. This could be a clue."

"A clue to what?" she asked as her brother tapped on the box some more. She was just about to tell him to quit it when she realized that Xander's finger-thumping sounded odd. "Hey," she said. "Do that again."

"Do what?"

"This." She reached over and thumped the box with her own fingers and their eyes met. "It's not cardboard like the rest. It sounds sturdier, like wood." She kicked it, and then said, "Ow!" It hadn't budged.

"It's full of something heavy." Xander gave it a shove. "*Really* heavy. Or it's attached to the floor."

Xena ran her fingertips over the edges, feeling for tape that she could peel off to open the box, and stopped on a corner. "What's this?" she asked.

Xander elbowed her aside. "It's a hinge!" He felt farther down the edge. "And here's another one!" He worked his fingers into the edge opposite the hinges and pulled. For an agonizing second nothing happened. Then the front of the box popped open. They stood back and stared at it.

"Well, that could explain the fake dust," Xena said. "Somebody must do something with this box that knocks the dust off it and they don't want it to stand out for some reason. The fake dust makes it blend in with the others."

They stepped closer and peered inside. They couldn't see much from that angle. Somebody would clearly have to crawl into it. "Go on," Xander said, gesturing at the opening.

"No, *you* go," Xena said, although she really would have liked to explore it. "You're smaller. I'd hardly fit."

Xander took a breath and crawled in. Almost instantly he bumped his head. "Ow!"

"Way to go, cowboy," Xena said. "Try not to knock yourself out in there."

"Oh, shut up," he muttered. He looked around. "There's nothing in here," he said. "Just the back of the box." He stopped. His eyes were adjusting to the semidarkness and now he could see that what he had bumped his head on wasn't the end of the box, but a wall. And it wasn't a plain surface. On it were four knobs, with lines radiating out from their centers. The holes on the top of the box that had looked like random damage were actually cleverly placed to allow light to fall on the knobs.

"Whoa," he said softly.

"What?"

Xander didn't answer. He reached out a hand.

23

The knobs looked exactly like the dials on a combination lock. The first three had numbers, and the fourth had letters of the alphabet instead. He rotated one, and it twirled jerkily.

"Xander, what *is* it?"

"It's knobs, like on a safe," he said. "Wait a sec. I think I might be able to come up with the combination."

He concentrated. Baker Street Irregulars. Sherlock Holmes had lived on Baker Street, at the most famous address in London, someone had once said. He relaxed, knowing that if he opened his mind, the exact address would come to him. Three numbers and a letter. Three numbers and a . . .

Yes, there it was. Flashing in front of his eyelids: 221B Baker Street.

It was just like the knobs. Three numbered knobs, and then a lettered one. Xander set the first two dials on 2. The third dial was already on 1, and as he twirled the fourth one, he felt a deep certainty. The dial stuck a little on its way to B. Then it lined up with a satisfying click.

Xander hesitated, nervous about what he'd find on the other side of the door. But there was no turning back now.

He pushed on the wall—and the small slab

of cement moved. He blinked in the bright light that hit his face, blinding him momentarily.

"What's that light?" Xena's voice was eager.

"It's a door!" Xander's voice was hoarse with excitement. "A door, Xena! We can get out of here!"

Xena was so relieved that her knees suddenly felt weak. "Oh, hooray! Where does it go? Back to the pub?"

But Xander couldn't answer, because he wasn't sure what he was looking at.

CHAPTER 4

Xena couldn't stand it anymore. She dropped to her knees and squeezed herself into the box. She poked her head through the opening just as Xander disappeared in front of her.

A burst of laughter greeted her. Startled, she looked up.

She didn't know what she was expecting, but it certainly wasn't three pairs of legs, one in jeans, one in a man's long pants, and the third in pantyhose and small flat shoes. "Who—" she started to say when a hand reached down and helped her crawl out. She stood up next to her brother, and they both stared around the room.

It seemed like an ordinary living room, with comfortable-looking chairs and couches, a few lamps, and a bookshelf. A colorful rug covered the floor, and weak afternoon sunlight was coming in through two broad windows.

Now that Xena and her brother were upright

they could see the people to whom the legs belonged. There was an elderly lady with a sweet-looking, wrinkled face, wearing a flow-ered dress. Xena thought she looked familiar but couldn't place her. Next to her stood a skinny, pale boy about Xena's own age with bright red hair. She also saw a short, balding man—the man who had helped her to her feet. His broad smile looked as though it was going to split his round face in two. And behind them stood a small crowd of maybe a dozen people, all smiling and clustered as if they knew one another well.

"Wait a minute! I know you!" Xander exclaimed to the round-faced man. "You dropped that paper into my sister's hand at the hotel!"

The man's smile grew even wider as he bowed to them. "Leroy Brown, at your service," he said.

"At our *service*?" Xena folded her arms across her chest and gave him a steely stare. "Who are you people? Why did you lock us in that room? And what do you want from us?"

"Yeah!" Xander said, but Xena could tell he was more excited than angry.

The redheaded boy rolled his eyes and sighed loudly. "Aunt Mary, can't we get on with this? I'm going to be late for football practice."

"Are you kidding me?" Xena was astonished. "You're part of a crime here—*two* crimes. They're called kidnapping and forced imprisonment."

"Oh, darling!" The elderly lady's face was pained. "We didn't kidnap you! It was a harmless lark. It was a kind of—" She waved her hands as though unable to think of the word.

"A test," Mr. Brown said. "And you passed with flying colors. You discovered which box was different, and you also figured out how to open it."

"A *test*?" Xander asked.

"Yes," said the redheaded boy. "They wanted to see if you were *worthy*." He left the group to sit in a chair by the fireplace. "Let me know when this is over," he grumbled.

"Worthy of what?" Xander asked.

"Oh, I should have prepared for this better," the lady said, looking at the others for help. "I don't really know where to—"

The boy broke in from the chair. "Aunt Mary," he said with another sigh. "Shall I do it? It will go much faster."

"Thank you, Andrew." The woman looked at him gratefully.

"The game you were playing this morning," the boy—Andrew—said, "the one where you sat on the steps of the hotel and guessed at the occupation of the people passing by?"

Xena nodded but Xander interrupted him. "How do you know what game we were playing?" he asked.

"Oh, never mind about that," Andrew said. "We have our ways."

"The doorman," Xander whispered to Xena. "He was close enough to hear us. But why would he tell these people about the Game?"

This was getting complicated.

"The doorman at your hotel is one of us," Mr. Brown said. "His great-grandmother was a detective as well."

"Now that we've got *that* cleared up," Andrew went on, "the *Game*," he said with such reverence that Xena and Xander could almost hear the capital *G*. "Didn't it seem familiar to you?"

"Of course," Xena snapped. "Our father plays it with us all the time. And he learned it from his father."

"Who learned it from his father, who learned it from *his* father, who learned it from *his* father," the boy finished. "Your great-great-great-grandfather," he added.

Xander mentally added up all the "fathers" and nodded. "Okay," he said. "But so what?"

"It was your great-great-great-grandfather's favorite game," he said. "Surely you've read about it."

"You forget," the old lady said. "Their parents never told them! Your great-great-great-grandfather," she continued with something new and serious in her voice, "was a very dear friend of my great-great-grandfather, whose name was John Watson."

So what? Xena thought, but Xander seemed suddenly thrilled.

The lady went on. "And your great-great-great-grandfather's name was—"

"Sherlock Holmes!" Xander turned a shining face toward Xena. "We're related to Sherlock Holmes! How awesome is that!"

"What?" Xena couldn't believe it. The most famous detective that ever lived was their how-many-greats grandfather? How could that be? Why wouldn't they have known it before?

"But how did you know that when we didn't?" Xander asked.

"Don't you remember me?" The old lady smiled, and suddenly Xander realized why she looked familiar.

"You came to visit us, didn't you?" he asked. The lady nodded, looking pleased. "When I was about three, right?"

Now Xena recognized her too. "Our father called you Aunt Mary," she said. "Are you our aunt?"

"Oh, heavens, no." The woman shook her head and wisps of gray hair fell out of the bun at the back of her neck. She tucked them in and went on. "I'm just an old friend of the family. Our families have been friends ever since my great-great-grandfather, Dr. John Watson, helped Sherlock Holmes solve cases. I'm Mary Watson."

"She's *my* aunt," Andrew said. Everyone ignored him.

"Sherlock Holmes and Dr. Watson!" Xander said. "Amazing!"

Xena broke into a wide grin. "This is so cool," she said.

"I'm happy you remember me," Aunt Mary said. "We've invited you here because your dear father, although a lovely man and *quite* talented, has never taken an interest in Sherlock's great work. I understand that as a boy he was teased for claiming the great detective as his ancestor. Perhaps that's why he never told you. But we've been keeping an eye on you in the United States.

31

We knew that you two were different, and we were thrilled to find out that you were coming to London!"

She looked inquiringly at Mr. Brown, who had been fiddling with a cabinet in the corner of the room. He stepped forward, holding a large leather-bound book in his hands. It looked old, and it smelled musty. Mr. Brown's face creased with a smile as he extended it to them.

If there was anything Xena couldn't resist, it was an old book. She held her breath as she reached for the worn volume. Stamped into the cover were the words *SH Cases: Unresolved*. She raised questioning eyes to the man.

"Oh, come *on*," Andrew said. "It contains the unsolved cases of Sherlock Holmes and Dr. Watson."

"Unsolved cases?" Xena repeated.

"Well, yes," Mr. Brown said softly. "Even your illustrious ancestor, the greatest detective who ever lived, couldn't solve *every* case that came his way. The scientific and technological limitations of the day, you understand."

"And sometimes he was called away on more pressing business," Aunt Mary added. "If his government needed him, he had to leave a case before finding the answer."

"But why are you giving this to us?" Xander asked, peering at the cover of the book, still clutched in Xena's hands. "Do you want us to solve the mysteries?"

"Ha!" Andrew snorted.

Aunt Mary shot him a stern glance. Then her face softened again as she turned to Xander. "No, dear," she said. "We would never ask you to do that. And I'm sure the trails have gone cold after all this time. It's just that it belongs to your family by rights, so we think you should have it . . . whether or not you set your minds and talents to solving any cases."

"Thank you!" Xena and Xander chorused. Xander had to hold himself back from jumping with excitement, and Xena felt as flushed as if she had just run a race.

Somehow they knew that this book was going to change their lives.

CHAPTER 5

Maybe we can solve some of the cases in the casebook," Xander said. Aunt Mary beamed at him and Xena.

"All our resources," said Mr. Brown, "are at your disposal. One of our members is a chemist, and he can help with analysis, and—"

"There's time for all that later," Aunt Mary said. "Now let's celebrate the newest members of the SPFD!"

"I think we'd better go," Xena said reluctantly. "Our mother is expecting us."

"Oh, we've already gotten word to her," Mr. Brown said.

"We've planned a small celebration, dears," said Aunt Mary. "All of us in the Society for the Preservation of Famous Detectives would like to welcome you to our little group."

Except for him, Xena thought as she watched the redheaded boy slip out a side door.

She didn't need to be a famous detective to know that Andrew Watson didn't like them one bit.

"When is it going to be *my* turn?" Xander asked his sister the next day. Xena was flopped onto her twin bed against the far wall and had been hogging the casebook for hours.

"Pretty soon," she said, but she seemed in no hurry to pass the book over to him.

Xander sat on a small chair by the window and stared out at the gloomy, rainy Saturday afternoon. He sighed and watched a raindrop hurry down the pane of glass and catch up with another one. He took his eyes away from the window. "I can't believe I'm so bored that I'm watching raindrop races," he said. "Is there anything in there we could try to solve?"

"I wish," Xena said. "But these cases took place over a hundred years ago. There's one about a ruby that somebody lost and then some weird notes about a toeless guy. Stuff like that. It's mostly just notes and sketches. I'll tell you if I find anything. Mom said we had to do something cultural this afternoon anyway, remember? Why don't you look for an art exhibit or something?"

Xander groaned and picked up the newspaper that was resting on a tiny wooden end table. During their first days in London their mother had made them go see the Rosetta Stone and huge landscape paintings and Greek sculptures, and Xander didn't want to go to another museum the whole rest of the year. But Xena was different. She could go to a museum every day for a week and then wake up the next day and ask to go to another one.

Xander scanned down the page. "Medieval illumination," he read. "Wire sculptures by some guy with a name I can't pronounce, paintings by Nigel Batheson, nature photographs—"

"What?" Xena interrupted him.

"Nature photographs."

"No, that other one," Xena said. "Paintings by who?"

"Nigel Batheson," Xander read again.

"Wow!" Xena said. "This is amazing! Look at this." Xander got up to join her, and she angled the casebook toward him. He peered at the old-fashioned handwriting as Xena took the newspaper.

"Nigel Batheson," Xander read aloud. *"Girl in a Purple Hat*. Noticed missing Thursday last." There were some more notes, and at the bottom of the next page was a notation in the same

Taynesbury

4 March 1907
Nigel Batheson—Girl
in a Purple Hat
Noticed missing Thursday last.

Leads:

Marguerite Batheson reports painting missing from home. Paintings were to go on exhibit in London and then sold. Nothing else missing from house.

Perhaps Ghastly children had birthday celebration on the 10th. Ghastly children destroyed it? (horrible creatures)

Family
Wife—Marguerite
Children—
Abner,
Cedric,
Robert

Model?

Batheson unduly fond of painting—who was little girl?

Painting was there on November 10th.

Note:
Manor house vacant until Xmas

Purple hat borrowed from neighbor's daughter—but she was not subject of painting.

handwriting but a slightly different shade of ink, as though some time had elapsed between the inscriptions: "Case abandoned to pursue intriguing problem of lion's mane."

They both sat back. "It's got to be the same guy," Xena said. "How many artists named Nigel Batheson can there be? And look—they even mention that same painting in the newspaper." She ran her finger down the column. "See? It says, 'Sadly, Batheson's most important work is still missing from the collection. This painting, *Girl in a Purple Hat*, is a portrait of a little girl of about eight seated on a wicker chair in a summer garden.'"

"What?" Xander broke in. "That's the same picture as in the notebook!"

"Duh," Xena said. "That's what I just said. Anyway, the paper says, 'The painting was discovered missing a century ago and has never been recovered. Fortunately, a copy had previously been made.' Look, there it is." They bent their heads over the newspaper. The grainy picture showed a pretty girl with blond curls and a bright purple hat, sitting on a chair with flowers and shrubs behind her. The contrast between the color of the hat and the girl's green eyes was striking even in the newspaper.

Xena went on reading. "'Although it is claimed that the copy could never capture all the charm of the original, at least it gives an idea of what the missing painting looked like. Note the model's slightly sulky expression, which makes the painting stand out from the sometimes overly sweet view of childhood frequently depicted in portraits of the era.'"

Xander sat back on his heels. "Wouldn't it be awesome if we could find that painting? I mean, isn't it amazing that we saw the name of the artist in the paper? It's like it was meant to be."

"That would be cool!" Xena said. "But it's been missing for so long. Where would we begin to look?"

"We have something that could help," Xander pointed out. "We have this." He gestured at the casebook. "The notes of the great Sherlock Holmes. They give us a head start. Look, here's a list of names. Wife—Marguerite; children—Abner, Cedric, Robert."

"And what does this mean, do you think?" he pointed at the word *Taynesbury* scrawled in a corner. A little farther down was a sketch of a dragon that seemed to be curled up on itself with its tail in its mouth.

Xena took the notebook from him. "I don't

know, Xan. Those names could be anything. And it looks like the dragon is just a doodle. It says that the painting was noticed missing on a Thursday. But that's not really a big help."

"Come *on*, Xena." Xander was impatient. "We've watched hundreds of mystery shows on TV and we always figure out the bad guy before the detective does. And I'm always reading detective books. Besides, we have Sherlock Holmes's genes. Doesn't that mean anything?"

Xena hesitated before answering. "It could be dangerous."

"Are you kidding?" Xander laughed. "Looking for a picture of a girl in a purple hat could be *dangerous*? How could finding the answer to a hundred-year-old secret be dangerous?"

Xena glanced down at the newspaper again. "We wouldn't have much time," she said, and Xander held his breath, knowing she was considering it. "The exhibit opens next Friday at a museum called the Victoria and Albert, and then a few days later it leaves on a worldwide tour. This guy Batheson has gotten really popular again all of a sudden, the paper says."

Xander nodded. "We owe it to him," he said, rubbing his finger over the initials stamped on the cover. "Not to Batheson. We owe it to our great-great-great-grandfather. He solved most of the mysteries he set out to solve. It's not his fault he had to leave this one before it was finished. Let's see if we can figure it out for him."

Xena looked at her brother. From someplace deep inside of her came a sense of family pride she hadn't known she possessed. Wouldn't it be amazing if they could solve some of the great Sherlock Holmes's cases for him?

She stood up. "Okay. Let's find that painting before the art show opens," she said. "Or at least before the exhibit goes on tour around the world. Let's make sure it's included this time, just as though Sherlock himself had found it."

Xander stood too and held out his hand. Xena took it and they shook on the deal.

"Now," said Xander. "Where do we start?"

CHAPTER 6

Good question, Xena thought. Maybe it was too tough a case. Maybe that was the real reason their great-great-great-grandfather had dropped it—not because a more urgent problem had popped up. What could two kids do where Sherlock Holmes had failed?

Xander didn't seem troubled by these doubts. "Okay," he said. "Let's make a plan. Go on, you know you're dying to make a list!"

Xena pulled out a piece of paper and ignored his tease about how much she liked to make lists. "First, let's find out everything we can about Batheson and his family," she said as she wrote, "1. Family."

Xander nodded. "Maybe we can find out where he kept his paintings and who could have taken one. And let's find out the model's name," he said. "Maybe she left a diary or letters or something that would help."

Xena wrote down, "2. Model's identity." She tapped the end of her pencil on the paper. "Let's see if we can take a look at any of his other paintings and drawings," she said. "Maybe we can find some clues."

"Good idea," Xander said. "And then what?"

"We'll just have to see what we turn up," Xena said.

There were some advantages to working in the modern day. One of them was the Internet. Xander tried to look over Xena's shoulder as she typed, and he accidentally jiggled her arm.

"Whoa, cowboy," Xena said as she pressed Print.

"Quit calling me that," Xander said, but she ignored him, as usual.

"First you have to listen to this stuff about Batheson," she said. "It's mostly about his paintings and not a lot about his life, but there's some pretty interesting information." The printer stopped whirring, and Xena took out the sheets and smacked them on the desk to even them up. "Okay," she said, settling on her bed, her long legs crossed in front of her.

"Number one. Nigel Batheson married a lady named Marguerite Sawyer. They had three sons. The family lived in the country, in

Hertfordshire, wherever that is, and they hardly ever had any visitors because Batheson was really shy. I think he had agoraphobia."

"Ah." Xander nodded. He'd seen the word in the dictionary. The definition popped into his mind. "Agoraphobia. Fear of open spaces, from the Greek words *agora*, meaning 'marketplace,' and *phobia*, meaning 'fear.' Now generally intended to mean fear of traveling away from familiar surroundings."

"Show-off," Xena said. "Okay, number two. When he died, his family was really poor, so his wife decided to sell some of his paintings. But when she went to get *Girl in a Purple Hat* out of storage in their home to send to a gallery in London where more buyers could see it, the painting was gone."

"Was anybody arrested?"

Xena riffled through the pages. "It doesn't say, so I bet not. Number three. The actual date of the theft remained uncertain because Mrs. Batheson said the picture was put into storage soon after it was finished and she hadn't gone looking for it until years later. The police questioned all the servants, but everyone denied knowing anything. One of the boys had grown up and gotten married, and the other two were away at boarding school. The police asked them all about it, but didn't learn anything there either."

Xander reached for the papers. He leafed through them and looked up. "No wonder this case was so tough. The painting could have been stolen long before anyone noticed it was missing." He dropped the papers back on the bed.

"True," Xena said. "That does make it harder."

"So now what?" Xander asked.

Instead of answering, Xena reached for the phone book and looked up *Batheson*. It was a long shot, but at least it was a place to start. She dialed the first number in the column. No answer. She dialed another number. This time it rang only a few times before a man picked up. Xander leaned in and Xena angled the phone so that he could listen too.

"Hello, Mr. Batheson?" she said.

"Speaking," a brisk male voice replied.

"Um, you don't know me, but my name is Xena Holmes."

"You're an American, aren't you?"

"Yes, sir," she said. "I'm—"

"I could tell from your accent," he interrupted.

Accent? she thought. I don't have an accent! He's the one with the accent! "I'm here with my family, and I was interested in finding out more about the painter Nigel Batheson. Are you related to him?"

"Yes, dear," the man said. "I am indeed. He was my great-great-great-grandfather. I never knew him, of course."

"Yes!" Xander whispered, pumping his fist in the air.

"I was wondering," Xena said, and then paused. She hadn't thought of what to ask next. Her eyes telegraphed a "Help!" to Xander.

"Ask him what his favorite painting is," he whispered.

"What's your favorite Batheson painting?" she asked.

"Oh, that's easy," he said. *"Abner at the Fair.* Abner was Nigel's son and my great-great-grandfather. Batheson didn't complete many paintings, and that's the only large oil of my ancestor. It's always nice to feel connected to a bit of history. Know what I mean?"

"Yes, I do," Xena replied, thinking of the casebook.

The man went on. "Nigel was a very with-drawn man, you know. In fact, a historian once said that the way the fair is painted in Abner's portrait is wrong for the time period. It would have looked old-fashioned even then. So Batheson must have painted his son in the garden and then added a fair he remembered from his own childhood as background." He chuckled. "People say we English people are eccentric. I don't know if that's true, but Nigel Batheson certainly was!"

This is good, Xena thought. Very good. She took a deep breath and tried to sound casual. "And the one with the girl—the missing painting?"

"Ah, yes," he said. *Girl in a Purple Hat*. A lovely thing, if the copies can be believed."

"Do you have any guesses about what happened to it?"

"Afraid not, my dear. Why, I can't even imagine who might have been the model!"

Now, that was interesting. If Nigel Batheson didn't have any daughters and if he didn't like meeting new people, who could the girl in the painting have been? Xena wondered.

Then she realized the man on the phone was saying something.

"I'm sorry?" Xena asked.

"I wanted to know if you had any more questions," the man said.

Xena turned to Xander, who shrugged. "Not right now," she said. "But may I call you back if I think of something else?"

"Certainly!" he said and hung up.

"Try another number," Xander suggested, but they struck out. There weren't many Bathesons in the phone book. A few weren't home and the others had never heard of Nigel Batheson.

"I guess we might as well give up," Xander said, not meaning it. He knew that once Xena set her mind to something, she wouldn't quit. Their father called her a bulldog.

Xena picked up the newspaper and scanned the About Town section again. "There's an art gallery that has some Batheson sketches. Let's check it out."

"Okay," Xander agreed. "And Mom will be thrilled that we did something cultural."

"I sure will!" They both turned around at their mother's voice. "What cultural activity were you planning on doing?"

While Xander explained, Xena jotted down the address of the gallery.

"That sounds fine. I'll walk you to the bus stop," their mother said.

"Oh, Mom . . ."

"Don't whine, Xander. I just want to make sure you don't get lost."

They all put on raincoats and stood at the bus stop in the drizzle. When the bus arrived, their mother got on with them and asked the driver some questions while Xena and Xander found seats and pretended not to know her.

"The driver will tell you where to get off," she called back to them with a big smile. "And you get the bus back on the other side of the street from the gallery."

"Fine, Mom, thanks!" Xena sounded as cheery as she could so that Mom would get off, and with a big wave at them, she did.

"I wish she wouldn't treat us like kids," Xander grumbled.

Although there weren't many of London's famous double-decker buses on the roads anymore, riding buses through the city was still fun. London was so different from home. Xander loved seeing old buildings right next to brand-new ones, and the neat-looking bulgy black taxicabs zipping around. He leaned his forehead against the window, looking out at the drizzly day. It was still confusing to ride on the left side of the street. Sometimes when they went around a corner he thought that the driver had gotten mixed up and they were going to have a head-on collision with another car.

People walked under umbrellas, wearing raincoats and boots. Everything was gray and dull—the raincoats, the store windows obscured by rain, the expressions on people's faces.

That was why, when a sudden flash of purple crossed his line of sight, he didn't even realize what it was at first. He was just surprised to see color. But then he focused more closely. Was it? Could it be? . . . Yes, it was!

"Xena!" he cried.

"Hush," she said. "Everybody's staring at you!" But Xander kept his eyes on the girl who was darting under awnings, dodging the raindrops, holding her colorful hat on her head with one hand. Even in the gray light of a drizzly day he could see that the ringlets under the hat were bright golden blond.

"Look!" he said, pointing out the window.

"What?" Xena asked.

"It's her!" Xander half rose from his seat. "It's the girl in the purple hat!"

CHAPTER 7

The girl from the painting? No way!" Xena swung around and looked where Xander was pointing. But the girl had vanished into a crowd, and when the bus passed the corner where Xander had last seen her, there was no girl and no purple hat.

"You're nuts," Xena said. "Or barmy, as they say here. I think you've lost what little mind you ever had, brother dear."

"But she was there! I saw her!"

"Xander, you couldn't have seen her. The model would be more than a hundred years old. You must have imagined it. Or you just saw some kid in a purple rain hat."

"It wasn't a rain hat! It was one of those hats with ribbons and flowers, like old ladies wear." Xander kept his nose pressed to the window, but it was no use. The girl was gone.

"This is our stop," Xena said, and Xander

got up and went through the door after her, stepping down into a puddle. Great, he thought as he followed her.

A bell tinkled as they opened the door to the gallery. The man at the desk nodded at them as they came in, and then went back to his newspaper. The gallery was a series of small rooms, with lights shining down on the drawings, all in dark frames.

In the Batheson room was a brochure that described the sketches, but it didn't provide much information beyond titles that were pretty obvious, like *Child Picking Roses*.

A few other people were walking around, either alone or in pairs, pausing at each picture. There weren't many.

Xena inspected a few landscapes, a drawing of boys playing with puppies, a pretty woman doing needlework, and the same woman gathering flowers.

Even though Xander knew he should be looking for clues, he wasn't really studying the art. Instead he kept thinking of that girl with the purple hat. He *knew* he wasn't crazy. He *had* seen her.

His boots squished when he finally moved on to the next group of pictures, and people turned to glare at him. He tried to walk quietly, but what could he do about noisy boots?

Then he heard Xena calling him in a loud whisper from three sketches away. "Check this out!" she said when he arrived. She was pointing at a card on the wall that gave information about the piece.

"Steeple of Church of St. Freda, Taynesbury, Herts.," it read.

"Hey—Taynesbury! That's the word in the notebook!" Xander's blue eyes sparkled. "What do you think it means?"

"I don't know," Xena said. "Maybe we could ask somebody."

They stopped at the front desk. The man looked up from his paper. "Yes?"

"Do you know anything about that painting that disappeared? *Girl in a Purple Hat?*" Xena asked.

"'Fraid not," the man said. "Nothing more than what it says in the art history books. I think the drawings are just as fine as the paintings, though."

"They are," Xena agreed. "But we were wondering about a couple of things."

The man looked inquiringly at her, so she went on. "Is Taynesbury the name of the town where the artist lived? And what does *Herts.* mean?"

"Yes, indeed," the man said. "He did most of his painting in Taynesbury. It's in Hertfordshire"—Xena and Xander noticed that he pronounced it *Harfurdsheer*—"which is abbreviated to 'Herts.' It's not far from London, although in the old days it would have been considered a good distance. Horses and carriages were quite slow, you know."

Xena and Xander thanked him as they walked out. Xander did a little dance on the sidewalk.

"Cut that out before someone sees you," Xena said.

He did, but he was still excited. "We already have a lead!" he said. "We know where he lived. Let's find out more and then see if we can get to that town."

"Mom and Dad will love to take us someplace outside of London," Xena said. "And there are bound to be even more clues at the museum where the Batheson exhibit is going to be next week—the Victoria and Albert. Let's go there next."

The street was crowded with people, and shop windows were bright in contrast to the gray sky. The sidewalks were narrower than what they were used to in America, and they constantly had to dodge people who were in a hurry.

Fortunately, the Victoria and Albert was nearby. "Hope they're still open," Xander said, and Xena nodded. They found the museum, though the sign on the door said it would be closing in fifteen minutes.

Inside, a guide was sitting at a desk, twirling a pencil with his fingers. The museum was practically empty.

"Hullo!" the man said with a wide grin. "You two must be real art lovers to come out in this wet!"

"Oh, I love art," Xena said.

"Anything in particular you want to see?" he asked. "You won't have much time. We're about to close for the day."

"We're interested in Nigel Batheson," Xena said. "We've looked at some of his work online, and I wanted to see it in person."

"Right this way." The man led them past a white wall with bright watercolors of fruit hanging on it. Then he stopped in front of a pencil sketch. "Well, here it is," he said. "Not much to see, I'm afraid. We're preparing his important works for the showing next week."

Xander examined the picture. It showed a little boy in a garden who seemed absorbed in cuddling a rabbit while behind him some adults and an older boy were sitting on the grass. It looked like a happy family picnic. "No girls in purple hats," he said.

The man laughed. "No, no girls. Batheson wasn't fond of strangers, so his only models were his wife and sons. He never painted girls, except in that one instance. People have always wondered who the model was. I'm not sure it matters, but it would be nice to find out, don't you think?"

Xena silently agreed with him and glanced at the wall. "Mostly I wanted to see his sketches for *Girl in a Purple Hat*," she said.

"Oh, those were destroyed," the man said. "This sketch here—like all of Batheson's sketches still in existence—is a study for a painting he never completed. It's interesting how he worked, actually. He made lots of drawings, sometimes more than a hundred, for each painting, and then he worked on the paintings for a long time. And when the painting was done, he would have the servants light a big fire in the drawing room, and he would burn the sketches."

"Why?" Xander asked.

"I think it was his own little ceremony to celebrate the end of the project," the man explained. "That's why the only drawings left are for paintings he never completed. If you could find a sketch for one of his finished paintings, a collector would pay you a lot for it."

"So, did he make many paintings?" Xander asked.

"No, he was a perfectionist," the man said. "He actually completed only fifteen oil paintings and a few watercolors. And now only fourteen of the oils are left. Luckily, we have them all here at the V&A."

"Except *Girl in a Purple Hat*," Xena put in.

"Right," the man said with a sigh. "It must have been a stunner. What a loss, when his collection is already so small."

The sun was setting by the time they left the museum, but at least it wasn't raining anymore.

"I can't believe we learned so much about Batheson already," Xena said. "Especially about him living in Taynesbury and that he burned his sketches." She glanced up at the cloudy sky. "I hope it'll be a nice day tomorrow. I don't want to do our entire investigation in the rain."

But Xander had more on his mind than the weather. "I wonder who that model was?" he said. "Maybe *she* took it. If we could find out who she was, then maybe we could find the missing painting!"

"Why would she take it?" Xena was intrigued at the idea.

Xander shrugged. "Maybe she wanted to keep it for herself?"

Xena considered this. "Or maybe she was shy about it being on display," she said. "If we could figure out who she was, we might be able to find out more about the painting."

"Let's see if Mom and Dad will take us to Taynesbury," Xander suggested. "They keep telling us they want us to see the real England, and Mom was talking about taking a car trip tomorrow anyway."

When they arrived at their hotel, the friendly doorman who knew Aunt Mary and the SPFD wasn't on duty. Instead it was the quiet one who acted as though letting them in was a big chore. The elevator had a sign on it saying OUT OF SERVICE so they had to walk up the three flights, with Xander's boots squishing at each step.

They found their mother in their room, sitting on Xena's bed with a map unfolded in front of her and guidebooks propped up on either side. Xander threw himself down next to her and pulled off his boots and wet socks.

"Just in time!" Mom said. "I have some great news. We found a place to live! It's not far from here. Dad and I will move our things into the flat on Monday, while you're getting to know your new school."

"Awesome!" Xena said.

"Now I'm trying to figure out a fun place for us to go tomorrow. I deserve a break after all this house hunting before I get back to work." She glanced at the corner of the room, where a bright yellow box waited. Xena and Xander both recognized it. It came from the product-testing company that their mom worked for, testing new gadgets.

"Anything good in there this time?" Xander asked, following her gaze. There'd been a video game that used some kind of new technology last time, and with any luck there would be something equally cool now.

"Just some cell phone," their mother said. "I haven't looked at it yet. We can bring it along tomorrow, and you can check it out in the car, once we decide where we're going. The problem is there's just so much to see. Help me narrow it down, will you?"

"How about Taynesbury?" Xena asked. "We were just at a museum with art by a man named Batheson, and he's from there." She left out the part about wanting to check out clues for one of

Sherlock Holmes's unsolved mysteries, in case Mom wasn't keen on the idea.

"Yeah," Xander added. "The place seems very educational."

"Taynesbury?" their mother said. "That's one of the places I was considering. It sounds charming." She flipped the pages in the guidebook. "It's a quaint little town that's supposed to look like the villages in the nineteenth century. And we can tour a mansion where King Henry the Eighth spent some of his childhood. Sounds like a good choice."

"Great!" Xena said.

"Oh, and by the way, Mary Watson called and asked if we could take her nephew Andrew with us tomorrow. She thinks you could all be wonderful friends."

Xena groaned and flopped onto the couch. "Not him, Mom! He's *such* a jerk!"

"Xena! How can you say that?" Mom asked. "You barely know the boy. I think Aunt Mary is being very nice, finding people your age for you to get to know." She gathered up her books and went back to her room through the connecting door. "Dinner soon," she said as the door closed behind her. "We're going out for curry tonight."

Xena loved Indian food, but who could

think about dinner now? Just yesterday she and Xander had been sitting around with nothing to do, and today they were on their way to cracking one of Sherlock Holmes's unsolved cases!

While Xander took the cell phone out of its shrink-wrap and read the manual, Xena's heart began to thump in anticipation. Tomorrow they'd do some *real* detecting!

CHAPTER 8

For the last time, stop crowding me," Andrew said, shoving Xander away.

"Why don't you leave my brother alone?" Xena told him. "He can't help it if the three of us are squished in the backseat."

"If I'd had my way, we wouldn't be," Andrew replied.

Me too, Xena thought. It was going to be tough trying to solve the mystery without Andrew butting in.

"I don't know why my aunt insisted I come along," Andrew complained. "I told her that I had better things to do than to go to Taynesbury."

"Like what?" Xander asked, leaning close to the other boy on purpose.

"Hey, hey!" Mrs. Holmes turned around in the front passenger seat. "No more arguing, please. Can't we have a nice conversation? We've got only about a thirty-minute drive."

Mom's right, Xena thought. We can be nice for a half hour. "Do you like detective books?" she asked Andrew.

He rolled his eyes. "Can't figure that out on your own, can you?" he asked. "Are you *sure* you're the descendant of the great Sherlock Holmes?"

"I know!" Mr. Holmes said from the driver's seat. "Let's play a memory game or a word game or—"

Andrew yawned. "No, thank you."

Xena thought about suggesting a license-plate game, but then decided against it. "So what's the deal with that phone?" she asked Xander.

"It has voice-recognition technology on it," he said. "No keypad. You speak the numbers into it."

"One point against it right there," his mom said. "What if you don't want someone near you to know what number you're calling?"

While her mother and Xander discussed the pros and cons of the new phone, Xena looked out the window. At least it's not raining, she thought, trying to stay positive. It wasn't exactly a bright, warm day, but soft sunlight fell on the hills. Almost as soon as they were out of the confusing snarl of streets and circuses—roads circling a monument—they were in the country. Or the suburbs, actually, but still, it was nice to be out of the noise and hurry of London. The road was narrow, and at times it was bordered by such high, thick hedges that it seemed as if they were driving through a tunnel.

"The next left," Mrs. Holmes said, checking the map and glancing up at the street sign. "Then right, then we should be in front of the mansion."

As they turned the final corner, Henry the Eighth's mansion appeared before them, and Xena's jaw dropped at the sight. The house was not only huge but graceful and noble-looking, sitting atop a lush green lawn. It was bigger than any house she had ever seen before, with two tall towers soaring above each side of the house. It was made of reddish brown stone, with windows that reached at least ten feet high. The windows were framed by the same white stone that made up the front steps.

"Nothing like this in the States, is there?" Andrew asked.

"Well, we do have the White House—" Xena started, but then she shrugged. "No," she said. "Nothing like this. Can we take a tour, Mom?"

Xena quickly lost count of how many rooms there were. Some had ceilings elaborately painted with fat little angels holding back painted curtains to show scenes of gods and goddesses. In other rooms, enormous fireplaces were topped by stone mantels covered with carvings of people hunting in the woods. They explored the grand staircase, the stained-glass windows in the private chapel, the portraits of grim-faced men and women lining the lofty corridors. The guide threw open a door. "This is where the future King Henry the Eighth played when he was a boy," she said.

"Imagine trying to play in here," Xander whispered to Xena. The room was huge and cold, with tapestries on the wall and hard-looking furniture.

"He probably had toys and things," Xena whispered back, but she couldn't help feeling a pang of sympathy for the little boy who'd tried to amuse himself in this formal hall, even though he'd lived and died centuries ago.

The tour ended in the same room where it had started.

"Let's go through the gardens now," Mrs. Holmes said. "They look lovely."

Xander grimaced. How could he and Xena get away to do some investigating?

"Now, don't make that face, Xander—" their mother began.

"Why don't we go into the village, and you can meet us there after the tour?" Andrew broke in. Xena looked at him in surprise. Did he actually want to spend time with them?

"I've been here on a school trip," Andrew explained. "There's a bus to the village at the gate."

"Great idea," Mr. Holmes said.

"Why don't you guys take the new phone, Xena," their mother said, handing it to her. "Call your dad's cell when you're ready to be picked up."

"Or we'll call you," their father said. "Or—"

"Dear, the garden tour's leaving," their mother said.

Mr. Holmes fished in his pockets and gave Xena a handful of bills. "Here, get yourselves something to eat."

On the bus Xena whispered to Xander, "While we're eating, make an excuse to leave the table and go find a phone book so we can check if any Bathesons still live in town."

"Got it," Xander whispered back.

The village was as quaint as their mother had said it would be—if "quaint" meant "really small and with not much to do." There was a narrow road with shops, some little houses, and lots of gardens. That was it.

They stopped in a tea shop where Xander ordered scones and clotted cream. Any food with *clotted* in its name didn't sound too appetizing, but that didn't stop him from eating the biscuits spread with soft cream until he thought he would burst. Andrew ordered something called bangers and mash, and even though she didn't know what it was, Xena ordered it too. I hope it's nothing weird, she thought, but fortunately it turned out to be sausage with buttery mashed potatoes.

Then Xander slipped away from the table while Andrew ordered another Coke. "No Bathesons in the phone book," he whispered to Xena when he returned. "And the waitress has never heard of them."

"What did you say?" Andrew asked.

Xena and Xander looked at each other. Maybe Andrew could help. Of course, he'd probably be obnoxious about it, but they might learn something anyway.

"We're working on a mystery," Xander said. Andrew snorted. "Well, we are," Xander went on. "It's about a missing painting—"

Andrew stood up, pushing his chair back noisily. They looked at him in surprise.

"What makes you think *you* can solve a mystery?" he hissed at them. "Just because your ancestor was the great Sherlock Holmes—" his voice dripped with sarcasm "—and mine was only Dr. Watson. Watson was as smart as Holmes. He was just too modest to write about himself. And all the movies about them make him out to be an idiot. Well, I'm sick of it." He smacked his hand on the table. "I'm going to that Internet café across the street. Come get me when it's time to go home." He strode out the door.

Xena and Xander looked after him in stunned silence.

"Wow," said Xena.

"Wow," agreed Xander. "Well, at least now we know why he doesn't like us. He's jealous that his relative isn't as well known as ours."

Xena took a deep breath. "We have to shake it off," she said. "Who knows when we'll be back here again? Let's find the Batheson house."

They paid for their meal and went outside. The wind had picked up a little, and it was chilly.

Xander pointed to a little stone church across the street. "I read somewhere that churches keep records about people. Maybe someone over there knows about the Bathesons," he suggested.

They crossed over to check it out. A note on the church's door said "Back at 3:00." It was 2:45, and with any luck their parents wouldn't call too soon.

Xander picked up a pamphlet. "Anything useful?" Xena asked.

"Nope," Xander said. "It's all about how old the church is and about the fine architecture of the nave, whatever that is, and about how some famous poet wrote a poem there. Nothing about people who lived here."

"Well, we might as well look around while we're waiting," Xena said.

The two took a stroll through the grounds and stumbled upon a small graveyard just off the back of the church. Many of the tombstones had flowers—some fresh and some plastic—leaning up against them. Moss had grown up over the markers, making a few impossible to read, and others were even less tended, sagging at odd angles as if the people buried there had been forgotten.

Xena hugged her sweater closer to her and read an inscription. "Emma Marsh. Died when she was just two years old. Sad." She glanced at the next headstone. "Winston Thompson. Beloved husband and father . . ."

Xena moved on to another marker and stopped.

"Xander!" she called. "Come back!"

Xander, who had been wandering across the churchyard, turned. When he saw Xena's expression, he broke into a trot.

"Look at this!" she said, pointing at the third headstone. "Another clue!"

CHAPTER 9

What is it?" Xander asked.

"Read it," she said.

He bent down. "Cyril Batheson. And he died only two years ago!"

"You know what this means?" Xena asked, almost whispering.

Slowly, Xander nodded. "It means that there are still Bathesons in Taynesbury. Or at least there was one, up until two years ago."

"Come on!" Xena said. "People usually bury family members near one another. Maybe there are more Bathesons here."

And there were, but they were all from long, long ago. Finally, just when they were about to give up, Xander spotted something. It was a headstone so small and overgrown with moss that they had already walked by it once. Xander squatted and scraped at the moss with his thumbnail.

"Sophie, daughter of Nigel Bath—" He almost stopped breathing.

Xena stooped next to him. "Keep scraping!" she said. But the rest of the stone had crumbled away under the moss.

"So maybe he *did* have a daughter!" Xena said. "She must have been the model!"

Xander nodded. "I wonder why she was never mentioned?" he asked. "Now we *have* to find some living Bathesons!"

At that moment the cell phone rang. As it tweedled out "Yankee Doodle," a woman placing a bouquet of flowers on a grave glanced at them curiously. Xena blushed and pressed the Talk button.

"Hi, Dad," Xena said. She crossed her fingers that their parents weren't on their way to pick them up.

"You kids doing okay?" Dad asked.

"Sure," Xena said.

"Can you three stand being on your own another hour or so? They're about to start a concert of Elizabethan music here."

Xena glanced over at Xander and gave him a thumbs-up sign. "Okay," she said. "We're touring an old church now."

"Excellent! We'll give you a call when we're

on our way over and arrange a place to meet."

"Okay," Xena said and hung up.

"Xander," she said. "We have an hour. What do we do now?"

"Wait a sec." Xander ran into the church. He came out a few minutes later with a piece of paper, which he waved at his sister.

"Directions to the Batheson house!" he called triumphantly. "I told the guy sweeping the floor that we were their distant cousins, and he told me that there's a lady here who was a Batheson before she got married. Her name is Mrs. Emerson now."

"How come the waitress had never heard of her?" Xena tried to grab the paper from him.

"Nuh-uh," he said, clutching it close. "I can get us there. Maybe that waitress isn't from around here. The guy said it's a short walk to the house. Let's go see if she knows something!"

"Okay," Xena said. "Just flash those dimples, and she'll answer whatever you ask."

Xander gave Xena a huge jack-o'-lantern smile and his dimples appeared. "I wonder if the painting is hidden at the house," he said as he trotted to keep up with his sister's long strides. "Maybe there's a studio. Hey, maybe he painted a picture over it and some innocent-looking painting has the purple-hat girl underneath."

"If he did, I wonder if the SPFD's lab could detect it," Xena said.

Xander said, "I don't think it's that hard. They X-ray it or something. But unless we really need the lab I want to keep the society out of it. I don't want that rotten Andrew knowing what we're doing."

They walked on a narrow lane with tall hedges on both sides. A Border collie ran out of a house and barked at them. Its tail was wagging, but there was an unmistakable warning in its eyes. Xena shivered.

"What?" Xander asked.

"Nothing," she answered. "Just cold."

Xander stopped and consulted his scrap of paper. He glanced at the gate in front of them. "Something's wrong," he muttered.

Xena snatched at the paper again and this time she was successful. "Number 76, Lilac Lane," she read aloud. "The Willows. What does that mean, 'The Willows'?"

"The guy said that's the name of the house."

"They name their houses here?"

Xander shrugged and looked at the house. "I guess so. But there's got to be some mistake." He hadn't been in England very long, but he could tell that this wasn't some historic mansion. It was a very small, very pretty, but very modern cottage.

"You're right," Xena replied. "This can't be the Batheson house. It's too new."

"Oh, but it is, young lady," a voice behind them said. They turned. A middle-aged woman was looking at them with sparkling green eyes. She opened the gate and let herself in. She didn't close the gate, but neither did she invite them in, and she kept one hand on the latch, holding a shopping bag in the other hand.

"Are you Mrs. Emerson?" Xena asked.

"I am," the woman said. "And what can I do for you?"

"We're doing a project on Nigel Batheson the painter," Xander broke in, giving the woman his best wide-eyed little-boy look. "We're going to a special exhibit of his paintings with our school, and our teachers will give us extra credit if we write a paper on him."

The woman beamed at Xander. Was it because he was so appealing, or was she pleased to talk about Nigel Batheson? Xena could understand that. She had found out only the other day that she was descended from Sherlock Holmes, and already she was proud of the connection.

"What do you want to know?"

"First," Xander said, "did he live in this house?"

"This house?" Mrs. Emerson looked amused. "No, of course not. His home was destroyed in the blitz."

"The what?" Xena asked.

"The blitz, during the Second World War." They must have still looked blank, because she went on. "We were bombed. The old house took a direct hit. Fortunately, no one was at home."

Xena felt her heart sink. If there were any clues in the old house they'd have been blown up with it. She wasn't about to give up though. We'll solve it, she silently promised her long-dead ancestor. We'll find the painting for you.

Xander decided to plunge right in. "We're mostly curious about that missing picture that Nigel Batheson painted, the one of the girl wearing a purple hat?"

"So are a lot of people, dear!" Mrs. Emerson said with a chuckle. She shifted the bag to her other hand. "I'm afraid there's not much I can tell you, and I'd like to put my shopping away."

"Do you have any idea what happened to the painting?" Xander asked anyway.

"Of course not," the woman said. "If I did, it wouldn't be missing, now, would it?"

"And what about Sophie Batheson?" Xena asked. "There's a gravestone in the churchyard that says she was Nigel's daughter. But he didn't have any daughters, did he?"

"Oh, that was my cousin Sophie," the woman said. "Her father was named Nigel Batheson after his own grandfather, the famous painter. Sophie died as a baby, poor lamb."

What a disappointment. The lady was turning away, and Xander said hurriedly, "And we were wondering who the model was."

With a *click* the gate slammed shut. "Sorry, love," the woman said. "But I have no idea, I'm afraid. I must get on with my chores. Good luck with your essay."

"But—" Xander began. Too late. She had gone inside the house, and the firm way the door closed behind her left no room for doubt about whether she was going to ask them in.

"Smooth move," Xena said.

"Well, I didn't hear you come up with anything better," he snapped.

"Don't get mad at me," Xena said. "We're no closer to finding the painting, and if we don't work together we're never going to solve this case in time for the Batheson exhibit!"

• • •

77

The sun was setting as they turned into the street that led to the Dulcey Hotel. They had dropped off Andrew first, and now it was late and everyone was tired. Dad let the two of them out at the front door of the hotel while he and their mom took the car back to the garage.

Then Xander saw something that made his heart stand still. "Xena!" he said. "Look! It's her again!"

Xena turned around with what seemed to Xander like maddening slowness. "Who?" she asked. "Where? What are you talking about?"

"There!"

"I don't see—" But then she stopped talking and just stared. A little girl with golden curls, a purple hat, and a long gray coat was sliding into a car. It sped off.

"See?" Xander said. "I told you she was real!"

CHAPTER 10

But if we have to go to school we won't *ever* be able to solve this case," Xander said.

"At least it's only half days for the first week." Xena was stuffing her pajamas into her suitcase so that their parents could move everything while they were at school. "And Sherlock had obstacles too. We'll figure it out." She sounded more confident than she felt.

Their mother came in and surveyed them. She straightened Xander's tie and pulled Xena's shirt collar out from under her sweater.

Xander stuck his finger inside his tie and tried to loosen it. No good. "Do you want to strangle me?" he demanded, but his mother just laughed.

"Most schools in England require uniforms," she said. "Even an international school. Personally, I think it's a great idea."

"You would," Xena muttered. They hauled

their suitcases outside and loaded them into the car. Xena looked down at her blue-and-green plaid skirt, thick leather shoes, and white socks. "Don't you ever tell my friends back home," she said to Xander as they settled into the backseat.

"I won't if you won't," he said.

"Deal."

They rode in silence for a few minutes. Xena saw Xander wipe his palms on his trousers. The Holmeses had never moved before, and she and Xander weren't used to being the new kids.

"It's okay," she said, as much to herself as to him. "Just wait till you get out on the soccer field and show them what you can do. They'll love you."

He gave her a tight smile, then turned to look out the window again.

Those were the only words they spoke until they pulled up in front of a building that looked like all the apartment houses around it: rectangular, plain brick, with big windows.

Mom got out of the car and climbed the stairs, pretending not to notice that they weren't following her.

"Well," Xena finally said. "It looks like we have no choice." They got out and trailed after her.

As Mom opened the door to the school, a

burst of noise and laughter greeted them. Three girls wearing the same uniform as Xena's went past, walking that stiff-legged walk that's as fast as you can go without getting yelled at for running in school. They shot curious glances her way.

The hallway was wide and the floor was made of polished brown wood. Lockers had lined the corridors in Xena's middle school, but there was nothing like that here. On the wall was a bulletin board with a map of the world and round-headed pins stuck into it. A large sign proclaimed OUR STUDENTS COME FROM EVERY CONTINENT EXCEPT ANTARCTICA!

From behind closed doors came the familiar squeak of chalk. A choir seemed to be rehearsing somewhere down the hall. Xena felt herself relaxing a bit. Maybe it wouldn't be so bad here. School was school, after all.

Then their mother beckoned to them, and almost before they knew what was happening, they had been introduced to a man who said he was "the head."

"Like the Wizard of Oz?" Xander whispered, trying to make his sister laugh.

But Xena wasn't in the mood and said, "No, dummy, like the headmaster, the principal."

Their mother signed some papers, then

turned to Xena and Xander. "Now, don't forget. You're going to our new flat after school, not the hotel, okay?"

They nodded, and then Mom told them good-bye, made sure they had their house keys and money for the ride home, and left.

A knock came at the door. "Ah, that must be your guide," the headmaster said. He called out, "Come!" and in walked Andrew Watson.

This has got to be a joke, Xena thought.

Andrew's welcoming smile vanished. He turned to the headmaster and said, "Are *these* the new kids you wanted me to take around?"

"Yes, indeed," the headmaster said. "Your aunt suggested it. Off you go now, and don't forget that you're to collect them at the end of the day and get them started on their way home."

"Yes, sir," Andrew said. He began walking down the corridor so fast that even Xena had a hard time keeping up.

Xander broke into a jog and said, "I thought this was an international school."

"It is."

"But you're English!"

"Right," Andrew replied. "My mum's from South Africa, and my parents want me to go to school with kids from other places. So they enrolled me here." And he didn't say another word as he dropped them off at their classroom doors.

The first day flew by in a whirl. The other students were clearly accustomed to newcomers, and most of them were friendly. Xena tried out for the choir, and the director told her that he was pleased to have another alto.

Xander planned to sign up for soccer tryouts the next morning. If he made it, he'd have his first scrimmage that same afternoon.

And since neither had studied foreign languages before, they were both put in the beginning Spanish class, which was taught by a young woman from Paraguay.

Xena and Xander didn't see Andrew again until the end of the day. He met them at the door.

"If you were real detectives," Andrew said, "you'd be able to find your way to the Tube without me."

Fine, Xander thought. He spotted a sign saying SUBWAY and headed for it.

"Where are you going?" Andrew called after him. "It's this way."

"No, it isn't," Xander called back. He went down the stairs at a trot and found himself in an underground pedestrian crossing. Oh great, he thought, and retraced his steps to where the other two were waiting.

"In England, a subway is a passage under a busy street," Andrew explained.

"No kidding," Xander muttered. He didn't want to look at Andrew to see if he was smirking, so he kept his head down as Andrew guided them to the right train. As it pulled out of the station, they saw him taking the stairs two at a time to get out of the station. At least they weren't going back to the hotel, but to their new flat with its high ceilings, big windows, and fireplaces.

As soon as they were in the door, Xander tore off his school jacket and threw it onto the floor. "Stupid thing," he muttered. "And why is there a giraffe on it?" Their mother had already explained to them that the school's logo reflected the founder's Kenyan origin, so Xena didn't answer.

Pretty soon Xander quit grumbling. "Let's get changed and start looking for that girl we saw yesterday," he said. "She's got to live around here someplace."

"What makes you think that?" Xena asked, unpacking her backpack.

"The first time I saw her from the bus, she

was walking right near the hotel, remember?"

Xena nodded.

"And the next time she was across the street. The hotel's only a few blocks away. We could go—"

"Sorry, but you're not going anywhere today," their mom said, coming in the door. "We've got a lot of work to do." They looked past her to the piles of boxes and suitcases.

Their search for the girl in the purple hat would have to wait.

The next morning Xander made the soccer team, but he wasn't sure if this was going to be a good thing. He hadn't played very well. He made it because only three boys tried out this season and Coach Craig *had* to take him. And even then the coach wouldn't give him a uniform until he promised to start calling the game *football*, not soccer. Worse yet, it turned out that the captain of the team was none other than Andrew.

Now that the school day was finally over, Xander was determined to make a better impression at the scrimmage. After all, back home he was the star of his team. He entered the locker room filled with guys changing into their uniforms and cleats, and took a seat next to a new player from Australia named Simon.

"Hey, don't worry about missing those goals this morning, mate," Simon told him. "You'll get better with practice."

"Thanks," Xander said and changed into a jersey with an emblem of a cartoonish giraffe on it. He and some team members filed out onto the middle of the field. Xander spotted Andrew, and his stomach twisted into a knot.

"I wasn't sure if the Yank was going to show," Andrew muttered to a teammate, just loud enough for Xander to hear.

The coach clapped his hands for attention. "Okay, Giraffes! I've arranged for us to scrimmage with a visiting team—the Knuckers."

"What's a Knucker?" Xander whispered to Simon.

"A legendary beast," Simon replied. "A sea serpent. There's a folktale about it scaring the farmers in the south of England."

"Oh," Xander said. A fierce sea serpent seemed way cooler than a dorky giraffe.

"This is just a practice game," Coach Craig told them, "but I still want you to play hard. Got it?"

"Right!" the team shouted. "Go, Giraffes!"

The two teams met in the middle of the field. The Knuckers wore bright green jerseys bearing the image of two scaly sea serpents, one blue, one yellow, battling on top of a gray shield. Xander thought the crest looked cool—and it kind of reminded him of something. Before he could figure out what, a whistle blew and the game began.

The Knuckers were as fierce as the legendary water monster they were named for. They stole the ball again and again, and drove in two goals. "Are you awake, Giraffes?" one of them called during a time-out. The others hooted.

Xander briefly had the ball before a short, chunky Knucker stole it from him. Darn! he thought. Next time I'll score!

But it was Andrew who scored the first goal for the International School. In the next play Xander ran fast as Andrew advanced the ball again. Xander cut to the left and positioned himself for a clean pass.

Andrew kicked it straight to him. "Get it, Holmes!"

A small crowd cheered from the sidelines.

Yes! Xander thought, ready to accept the ball. He pictured smacking it with his foot. He imagined watching it flying into the Knuckers' goal. He set up the kick—and a flash of purple caught his eye.

He lost his concentration. It was just for an instant, but that was enough. In the flash when he saw the girl in the purple hat passing by the field, a Knucker intercepted the ball and disappeared down the field.

A moment later the Knuckers scored another goal. The International School never really recovered. They scored one more goal, but lost 4–2.

As the team straggled off the field, Xander heard Andrew talking to Zafir, a Turkish boy who had scored the Giraffes' second goal. "That's what happens when you allow Yanks to play," Andrew was saying.

Xander clenched his fists. He burned with shame. Not only did that girl keep appearing and disappearing mysteriously, but he'd lost the game for his new school because of her! The next time she showed up, he vowed silently, he wouldn't let her escape.

CHAPTER 11

The next day was cold and drizzly. As Xena and Xander emerged from the Tube after school, they opened their umbrellas and trudged toward home. The few blocks hadn't seemed like much before, but Xena's backpack was heavy with homework and Xander was still sore from yesterday's soccer match.

"Want to play the Game?" Xena asked.

Xander looked around. The people on the sidewalks were walking fast, heads down and half hidden under umbrellas, raincoats dripping. "I don't think we can in this weather."

"Then how about a snack?" Xena fingered the change in her pocket. She had figured out English money by now and thought that she had enough. Maybe after a little food they could concentrate on the case.

Xander brightened and Xena hid a grin. The mention of food always cheered him up. "There's a place around the corner with amazing scones," he said. "Mom and I went there a couple of times when we were staying at the hotel and you and Dad were sleeping late."

Xena had been thinking more of something like fish and chips, but it was nice to see Xander looking eager for something instead of brooding about soccer. So she agreed.

They sat by the window and hung their wet things on hooks by the door. It was warm and bright in the café, and as they watched people hurry by in the semidarkness with their faces ducked against the rain, they felt very cozy.

The waitress said, "Oh, it's the American boy!" She smiled at Xander as he flashed her his killer dimples. "Scones and clotted cream?" she asked, and laughed at his eager "Yes, please!"

"And some cocoa too, please," Xena added.

The cocoa warmed their bellies as Xander spread cream and jam all over his first hot scone.

"There are only two days until the Batheson exhibit opens," Xena said. "We've *got* to find out something else." Xander nodded and took a huge bite.

"So what's our next step?" she went on.

Instead of answering, Xander sat upright, his mouth full of scone, and pointed out the window.

He spluttered something that Xena couldn't understand.

"What?" she asked, peering at the mist. But just as she caught a flash of purple, Xander bolted out the door, leaving behind his raincoat, umbrella, everything. Even his scones.

Xena slapped some money down on the table, hoping it was enough, and then took off after her brother. She ran out the door, barreling into a fat man who said, "Here now, young lady!" She caught her balance, blurted "Sorry," and dashed onto the sidewalk.

The crowd of pedestrians had thinned a little, but people were still blocking her view. Thank goodness the drizzle had stopped, though the visibility was poor in the misty air. Where's Xander? she thought in a sudden panic. And what made him take off like that? There could be only one explanation, she realized. He must have seen that girl.

She looked left, then right, standing on tiptoe on the step of a small shop to peer over heads through the darkening afternoon. Nothing. What will I do if I can't find him? What if— Then she saw him a block away, tearing down the sidewalk, barely missing other pedestrians, and she chased after him.

People stared at her as she splashed through puddles and dodged around lampposts. She hadn't run track since last year at school, and she was afraid of slipping on the wet pavement, but even so her long legs ate up the distance between them. She caught up to Xander and grabbed his upper arm to get his attention. He barely slowed.

"Where did she go?" Xena asked, panting.

Xander pointed wordlessly down a narrow street lined with brightly lit shops, and Xena took off again. She didn't see a purple hat or anyone with golden curls but she kept going. When she reached the corner the light was red, and she leaned over with her hands on her knees, waiting for the light to change, trying to catch her breath.

Xander could not keep up with his sister's long strides. He saw her stop at a traffic light up ahead, but when he reached the corner, she was gone. He peered in all directions, and then finally spotted her standing under an awning. She had her back to the brick wall of a building and was leaning sideways, peering through a plate-glass window where paintings and sculptures were displayed under bright lights. When she caught sight of Xander, she beckoned him to come closer.

"She went in here!" Xena said. "I'll go in and

see if I can find her. You go around back and guard the emergency exit in case she comes out that way." Xander nodded, and slipped around the building.

Xena hesitated. She must look awful, with her dark hair plastered down, mud splashed on her white school socks, and her navy blazer dripping wet.

Just as she was about to enter the shop, Xander appeared at the corner of the building. He gestured wildly for her to follow him.

"What?" Xena said as she joined him in the alley behind the store. "What if she comes out while we're back here?"

Xander had climbed up onto a trash can that was leaning against the wall. It wobbled and Xena grabbed on to it to steady it.

"Get down from there and let me do it," Xena said. Xander jumped down and she easily hoisted herself up onto the trash can and looked into the window above.

Xena gasped. What she saw was so unexpected that she couldn't take it all in at once. She closed her eyes and opened them again.

It was still there.

CHAPTER 12

If all that had met Xena's eyes had been a girl in a purple hat sitting on an old-fashioned chair, she wouldn't have been surprised. Curious, maybe, but not surprised. Instead she saw a roomful of girls sitting on chairs in bright gardens, the same sulky expression on each chubby face, the same blond curls spilling out from under each broad-brimmed purple hat. Girls in frames, girls on stretched canvases, girls in purple hats all over.

The room was filled with copies of the Batheson painting!

The girl they had been following was perched on a stool. A woman entered the room and inspected her, removed a cloth from an easel, and then dipped her brush in paint and got to work. A good deal of the painting was already done; all that was left to do were the girl's shoulder and face.

Xena turned away from the window and dropped silently to the ground, her knees flexing to take the stress of the landing.

"Now what?" Xander asked. "We can't let her escape again."

Xena nodded. "Come on. We're going into that gallery." They went around front and entered.

They were soaking wet, and Xena's clothes were dirty where she had scraped against the brick. The receptionist, a slender woman with white blond hair and fingernails so long and curved that it must have been impossible for her to dial a phone or type on a keyboard, looked in horror at their feet on the white carpet.

Xena shifted over to the hardwood and nudged Xander to do the same. "Quit pushing," he said, but he moved.

"Can I help you?" the receptionist asked.

"Er," Xander said.

"Just looking," Xena said.

"Looking?" The woman clearly didn't believe them. "Looking for what?"

"A present," Xander said.

"For our dad," Xena added.

"There are brochures by the door," the lady said, and then she turned her attention to the phone that was ringing in a soft double trill. Xander watched in fascination as she stabbed at the blinking light with a pencil eraser. So that's how she did it! But how did she type at the computer with those claws?

Xander was looking at the prices of the artworks. "Holy smoke," he said, using one of their father's favorite expressions. "Ten thousand pounds? For *that*?" He was looking at what appeared to be a lump of gray glass with pieces of metal sticking out of it. "What is it, a paperweight?"

"It's a piece by an up-and-coming Romanian glassblower," the receptionist said severely, hanging up the phone. "And now, if you have no questions—"

But at that moment the door burst open, and a young man, almost impossibly tall and thin, strode in, waving his arms.

"You still haven't sold a single piece of mine? Do you have my work stored here like in a . . . in a . . . in a warehouse?"

"Please, Mr. Georgescu," the woman said, rising from behind her desk. "Please, Mr. Georgescu, calm yourself."

"Calm myself!" His arms waved even more frantically. Xena and Xander looked at each other and nodded. They slipped through the door behind the receptionist's desk.

They found themselves in the room Xena had seen through the window—the one with all the copies of *Girl in a Purple Hat*. The artist was sitting with her back to them, but the little girl glanced up as they stopped at the door. Her eyes widened.

"Someone's here, Annie," she said.

"Hush, Sarah," the woman said. Her voice sounded odd, and Xander noticed that she was clenching a paintbrush between her teeth. "Just hush one second while I get your mouth. It's almost right but I think . . ." Her voice trailed off as she dabbed at the lips of the girl in the painting, turned down in an irritable expression.

"There!" she said, putting the paintbrush aside. "Another one done in time for the opening! And is that Miss Selden with our tea? Miss Selden, aren't you a bit early?"

She turned around. When she saw them, her face showed surprise. "Who are you kids?" she asked, reaching for a cloth. She wiped her hands, leaving smears of color on the rag.

Xander looked at Xena. Xena looked at Xander.

"We're detectives," Xena said. The girl on

the chair let out a hoot of laughter, and Xena turned to her. "Yes, we are," she said firmly. "We're detectives, and we've been looking for a missing painting."

"A missing painting?" the artist asked, removing her smock and hanging it over the back of her chair.

Her obvious amusement stung Xander, and he said, "It's a painting that's been missing for a hundred years."

"You mean *Girl in a Purple Hat*?" she asked.

"Aha!" Xander cried. "How did you know what painting we were talking about?"

"Isn't it obvious?" The artist waved her hand at the walls, which were covered with copies of the painting. "Why else would you come to this studio?"

"Why indeed?" asked a voice behind Xena and Xander.

They turned around. It was the receptionist, Miss Selden, and she was carrying a tray with a plate of cookies, a little teapot and mug, and a glass full of something fizzy.

"Tea!" the girl said, hopping down from the stool. She grabbed the glass off the tray.

"Careful!" the artist warned. "You don't want to stain that dress."

The girl put down the glass, and the woman helped her into an artist's smock to cover the dress. Then the girl reached up her hand.

Xena and Xander gasped. When the girl took off her hat, the golden curls went with it!

CHAPTER 13

Xena stared as the girl casually placed the hat with the curls attached to it on a chair and shook out her straight brown hair.

"That's a wig!" Xander blurted out.

"Children!" Miss Selden was obviously starting to lose her temper, but just then a bell jangled in the outer room. It sounded as though someone had come into the studio.

"It's all right, Mary," the artist said, pouring a cup of tea. "I'll handle this."

Miss Selden nodded and placed the tray on a low table near the artist's chair. Then she left, glancing back at them as she closed the door behind her.

"Don't mind her. She's a bit overprotective of the gallery," the woman said, stirring her tea. "All the same, it *is* a little strange, isn't it? The two of you bursting in here, soaking wet and bedraggled?" She took a sip of her tea.

"Sorry," Xena said, "but we're trying to find out what happened to *Girl in a Purple Hat.*"

Xander nodded quickly. "When I first saw this girl I couldn't believe it—she looked just like the one in the painting! I knew she wasn't the same girl, but it made me curious. I thought she might have something to do with its disappearance."

"How come you're making copies of the painting?" Xena asked.

The artist smiled, and friendly-looking crinkles appeared around her eyes. She stood up and opened a file cabinet, rummaging around among papers.

"Well, I don't know anything about the whereabouts of the real *Girl in a Purple Hat,*" she said. "I wish I did! I'm just making these copies to sell at the Batheson exhibit that opens on Friday. You know, as souvenirs." She pulled out a letter from the cabinet and handed it to Xander. It had an impressive-looking seal at the top with the Victoria and Albert Museum logo.

Xander scanned the letter. "So you have permission to make copies of it?" he asked.

The woman nodded. "I make sure to change some details so that nobody can be fooled into thinking it's the real thing. See, my girl has brown eyes instead of green. My niece, Sarah, is the model."

"Oh," Xena said. "But how come we've seen her all over this neighborhood wearing the costume?"

"I use a photograph of the picture to paint the background," the artist went on. "But I need a live model for the expression. I still don't think I have it just right, but it's better. Sarah lives nearby, so she comes here after school most days. She puts on the costume before she comes to get used to wearing it."

"The dress is scratchy," Sarah chimed in, "and the wig is hot."

"Yes, dear," her aunt said patiently, as though she'd heard it all many times before. She turned back to Xena and Xander. "Anyway, I expect that's why you've seen her before."

Refusing the offer of tea, Xena and Xander left the gallery. It had stopped raining, but that didn't help their mood any. They went by the tea room to pick up their things and then headed for home.

"Well, that was a dead end," Xander grumbled, kicking at a soggy piece of newspaper on the sidewalk. It clung to his boot and he hopped on the other foot, pulling the paper off and dropping it in a trash can. "We're never going to find the painting. We only have two days left!"

"Come on," Xena said, trying to look on the bright side. "At least we know that the girl in the purple hat has nothing to do with the missing painting, right?"

Xander nodded. "Right."

"So now that we've eliminated her we can stop being distracted and concentrate on getting other clues," Xena went on. "There's that dragon drawing in the casebook. We still don't know if it's just a weird doodle or if it means something. Let's see if we can track it down."

Back at home Xena picked up the casebook. As she flipped through the pages looking for the drawing of the dragon, something caught her eye. She turned the book sideways.

"Read Batheson's letters," said the words near the edge of the page. She looked at Xander. "Okay," she said. "It's almost like he's telling us what to do next."

The following day they were dying to get to the library down the road from their school to look for Batheson's letters. But Xena had to research migratory habits of birds in northern Europe for

Suspects??

- Talk to Mrs. B. tomorrow noon
- Kids?
- Housekeeper – Blasted woman won't talk!
- Gentleman next door is an artist, too?

Batheson's wife wants to paint Dr. Watson – Rubbish!

Meet Watson at Kings Arms – best fish and chips around!

Read Batheson's letters. Storage room locked?

There is nothing more deceptive than an obvious fact!

Kept key under flowerpot – how obvious.

Case abandoned to pursue intriguing problem of lion's mane.

SHERLOCK HOLMES · 221b BAKER STREET · LONDON

a report before she could work on the mystery. Their parents had been firm. "School first," they said. "Everything else can wait."

So it was up to Xander. While Xena looked for books in the ornithology section, he sat down at the computer nearest to her and typed "Batheson" into the "author" blank on the library page.

Only one name came up. It was "Nigel et al."

"Xena?"

"What?"

"What does 'et al.' mean?"

"It's short for 'and others' in Latin."

"Look at this," he said, and she came and peered over his shoulder at the screen. She tapped a few keys and more information came up.

"The letters!" she breathed.

"They're on microfilm," Xander said. "What's that?"

"I don't know," Xena said. She was itching to get to work on the case, but she knew she couldn't yet. "Can you go find out? I'll finish up as soon as I can."

Thirty minutes later Xander was absorbed in the Batheson letters, carefully lining up the small plastic films in the viewer the way the librarian had showed him. He jumped when he heard Xena's voice behind him ask, "Find any-thing?"

"Not yet," he admitted. "These people wrote letters. I mean, they *really* wrote letters. Like every day. Long ones. They've been copied onto these little sheets, and you have to view them here." He pointed at the screen.

"Really?" Xena slid into the seat next to her brother. "Move over."

Nigel Batheson hadn't written many letters, and they were mostly orders for paint and brushes and canvas, but his wife had. She had a sister in London, and her husband's reluctance to travel meant that they didn't see each other very often, so they wrote frequently.

"Lucky for us they didn't have e-mail yet!" Xander said.

Mrs. Batheson wrote a lot about her boys. Abner, the oldest, was quiet and studious. Cedric, the second, had a talent for music. And little Robert was always getting into mischief. "Robbie wouldn't sit still for his portrait," the mother wrote. "Nigel was quite put out with him and threw down his brush. He said that he should not have a portrait after all. Robert then put a toad in Miss Bailey's bed"—Miss Bailey, it appeared, was the governess—"and he gave away his shoes to a beggar boy he met in the lane. I have no doubt that the child needed shoes, but I would not be amazed if his father sold them for drink."

One by one the boys went off to school. They wrote letters home every week, but didn't really say much. Xander did some quick mental math with the date on the letters. "Boarding school when they were seven?" Xander asked.

"I guess they do that in England," she said. "Like Hogwarts."

Another letter mentioned that the boys had been ill. Cedric had nearly died of smallpox. He had recovered, "but I fear that his dear little face will never be the same," read the letter from his mother to her sister. "Yet I am thankful every day that the Lord has spared my sweet boy."

Cedric returned to school and things went back to normal. The headmaster wrote letters home about the boys, generally complimentary. But Robert was still getting into trouble. He put a toad in the bed of the boy upstairs from him, the headmaster said.

"Robert had a thing for putting toads in beds," Xander said. "I like him the best."

"You would," Xena answered.

A church bell outside rang. "Time to go,"

Xena said. "These letters aren't any help, and anyway, you've got soccer practice. I'll wait for you and if there's time when it's over we can come back to the case."

"Great." Xander's stomach twisted. He didn't know if he wanted to face his teammates. Back home everybody would have known that he hardly ever made mistakes and that next time he'd be a star again, but nobody here knew that about him. It stinks being a new kid, he thought as he trudged down the sidewalk.

Back at school he took his time changing. When he got outside, the boys were already playing on one field and the girls on the other. He spotted Xena near the bleachers with some girls in her class, watching the boys run a drill.

Xander bent down to retie the laces on his soccer shoes and heard Coach Craig's voice.

"Holmes!" he barked.

"Yes, sir?"

"Go over there." He pointed to the far end of the field. "Watson is going to give you some pointers."

Xander's heart sank. Please, not that know-it-all Andrew. Maybe there was another kid named Watson. No such luck. In the corner of the field stood an unmistakable figure, tall and skinny, with bright red hair, both hands on his hips and one foot balanced on a soccer ball.

"Come on," Andrew said. "I have a lot to teach you and not much time."

Andrew, surprisingly, was a patient teacher, and after an hour or so Xander started feeling the stirrings of confidence as he managed to dodge around the older boy and score a goal in the imaginary net behind him.

"Good job!" Andrew said, raising his hand for a high five.

Xander slapped the older boy's hand and threw himself onto the grass, panting. "Who are we playing next week?" he asked.

"The Knuckers again," Andrew said and laughed as Xander groaned loudly. "This is our chance to get even," he added. "You'd better practice."

Xander walked a few yards away to pick up the jersey he had tossed aside during practice. I wonder why he's being so nice? he thought.

"Ready to leave?" Xena asked, coming up alongside him. "How did it go with Andrew?" she said in a low voice.

"Not bad," Xander said. "Maybe since he's helping me he doesn't feel like the Watsons are so unimportant."

While Xander ran back into the locker room, Xena dug into her backpack to check for Tube fare. As she opened her wallet, a few papers fluttered away. The wind picked them up. "My pictures!" she cried.

Andrew, who was chatting with some guys nearby, heard her, turned around, and grabbed two pictures as they sailed past.

"Your dog?" he asked as he handed her a photo of Sukey, their basset hound.

Xena nodded. "Our cousins are taking care of her until we go home."

"Who's this cute little girl?" he asked, holding up another.

"Little girl?" Xena was puzzled. She looked at the snapshot Andrew was holding.

"Oh, that's Xander!" she said. "He played a daisy in his preschool play." In the photo, a chubby-faced Xander stood with a circle of white petals around his head. "I'm a daisy, I'm born in the spring, I burst from the ground when the birdies sing," she recited in a high-pitched baby voice.

"Hey, cut it out!" Xander came back to the field just in time to hear his sister recite the last lines of his part. He made a grab at the picture, but Andrew held it above his head.

"You want this?" Andrew asked, lowering it a little. "Be a nice little flower girl and maybe I'll give it to you."

Xander leaped at it again and this time he got it. And he'd been thinking that Andrew might not be so bad after all! But Xander's first impression had been right—the guy was a jerk. Xander started to tear up the picture.

"Hey, that's mine! I need it to remind me of when you were a nice little kid and not a pain." Xena tried to snatch it from his fingers, but Xander pulled it away.

He looked at it again, then slipped the photo into his back pocket. It was humiliating. No *way* would it ever see the light of day again. Xander would make sure of that.

On the way home Xena said, "I'm sorry about showing Andrew the picture," she said. "I didn't know you were still mad about that daisy costume."

No answer. He just stared at the floor for the rest of the ride.

"At least he said you were a *cute* little girl," she pointed out as they reached the front steps of their building. Still no answer. She unlocked the door and let herself in. She turned to close it again but Xander wouldn't move. "What are you doing?"

Xander stood frozen on the doorstep. His mouth hung open and his eyes looked dazed.

"Xander!" Xena was worried. "What is it?"

He blinked as though waking up.

"I have it, Xena!"

"You have what?"

"I think I know who the girl in the purple hat was!"

CHAPTER 14

Xena reached out and pulled him in, then slammed the door shut against the evening chill.

"What are you talking about?" she asked.

"We need to make a list," Xander said. "See if you make the same deduction."

Xena found a piece of paper and drew a line down the middle, dividing it neatly into two columns, the left-hand one headed *Clue* and the right-hand one *Deduction*. She passed it to Xander.

He wrote in the Clue column, "We thought Sarah looked like the girl in the missing painting but when she took off the hat and the wig she didn't." Under Deduction he wrote, "The girl in the Batheson painting didn't necessarily look like the model who posed for it either."

"So?" Xena asked.

Xander ignored her. "Clue: Little kids don't look especially boyish or girlish. Flower petals around the head of even a very masculine little boy make him look like a little girl."

"Very masculine?" Xena hooted.

"Shut up," Xander said and kept writing. "Deduction: The model for the painting wasn't necessarily a girl."

"Ah," Xena said. She saw where he was going and it made sense.

"Clue." Xander paused, then wrote, "All of Nigel Batheson's children were boys. He was very shy and didn't talk to people outside his family. He would never have had a stranger pose for him, even a kid."

Xander put down his pen and leaned back. "When you have excluded the impossible," he said, quoting Sherlock Holmes, "whatever remains, however improbable, must be the truth." He locked eyes with his sister.

"The girl in the purple hat," Xena said slowly, "was a boy?"

Xander nodded. He wrote in the Deduction column "The model was either Abner, Cedric, or Robert Batheson!" He sat back.

Xena pulled out the newspaper clipping about the Batheson exhibit from her desk. She and her brother studied the copy of *Girl in a Purple Hat*. True, they couldn't tell for sure from just the face. The green eyes could belong to either a boy or a girl, and so could the rosy cheeks and the pouting mouth. But the model appeared uncomfortable. Was the dress scratchy, like Sarah's? Or was it because the model was a boy who didn't want to wear a dress?

"I think the real clue," Xena said slowly, "is in the expression. If most portraits from that time make children look"—she consulted the clipping again—"look overly sweet, why did Batheson make this one look as grumpy as you did when Dad told you that you couldn't quit the soccer team?"

Xander ignored her. "The problem is, this doesn't really help us figure out where the painting is. Even if the model was one of the Batheson boys, so what? We don't have any more clues that will help us find the painting in time for the art opening tomorrow."

"That doesn't mean we should give up," Xena said. "We're on to something, Xander! When we go to the opening we're bound to see some of his descendants. I'm sure we'll find more clues there."

"What do you wear to an art opening anyway?" Xander asked.

"Black," Xena said promptly. "Whenever you

see people on TV at something like this, they're always wearing black."

Xena had tried on everything in her closet before finally settling on a pair of black jeans and a matching turtleneck. Now, as they waited to get into the Victoria and Albert Museum, their parents were chatting with a woman who had tattoos on both arms and a man with so many piercings in his ears, nose, lips, and eyebrows that he looked like a porcupine. I guess it doesn't matter what you wear to these things, Xena thought.

Xena and Xander checked their coats, then wandered around admiring the paintings and trying not to stare at the blank space on the wall representing the missing *Girl in a Purple Hat*.

Xander nudged Xena and pointed at something in the brochure. "It says that the artist made the frames himself out of wood and then they were covered in gold leaf—really thin sheets of gold. That's so cool!"

Xena wasn't interested in frames, gold-covered or not. She was scrutinizing the people. The artist they'd met on Wednesday was there with her niece, Sarah, who was wearing her "girl in a purple hat" costume. Sarah waved at Xena, who smiled and waved back. Then Xena spotted

Mrs. Emerson, the lady they had met in Taynesbury. She was over in a corner, talking to a group of men. Xena was curious. Maybe they were talking about the missing painting. It was a long shot but worth a listen.

She weaved along the edge of the crowd toward Mrs. Emerson's group. The plan was to get close enough to eavesdrop without getting caught. She could usually blend in without people noticing her. Her mother called this talent "Xena's cloak of invisibility." Xander called it nosiness. Whatever you called it, it would come in handy now.

But they weren't saying anything particularly interesting, just talking about how bad the traffic had been, and wasn't the weather awful, and what were they planning to do for Christmas. Xena looked at the men out of the corner of her eye. They shared a resemblance to one another and to Mrs. Emerson, especially their bright green eyes. They had to be Batheson descendants.

"What are you doing?" Well, that was the end of her invisibility. Nobody could help noticing Xander, especially when he didn't even try to keep his voice down.

"Nothing anymore," she said. "Now that you blew it."

"Why, it's those children," Mrs. Emerson said.

"The ones who were looking for great-great-grandfather's house. They're doing a school report on him. You children must be real art lovers!"

"We are," Xena said. "Especially when it comes to Nigel Batheson. I'm Xena Holmes, and this is my brother, Xander."

"Are you the kids who called me a few days back?" asked one of the green-eyed men.

Xena nodded. "Yes," she said. "We were disappointed not to be able to see the house he lived in."

"So much was destroyed during the war," said a man who was clutching a drink. "Such a tragedy. A lovely old farmhouse, reduced to rubble."

"No, the *real* tragedy is that Nigel Batheson's collection is incomplete." Mrs. Emerson pointed at the blank space reserved for the memory of *Girl in a Purple Hat*. "It's so sad."

"True, true," one of the men agreed.

"It's a shame the world will never get to study his greatest work," the tall one said. "Even the identity of the model is a mystery."

"We think we know who the model was!" Xander piped in. "Or at least we think we know who it *wasn't*."

Xena nudged Xander with her elbow. It was only a theory, after all.

"Whatever can you mean?" asked Mrs. Emerson. "How could you kids know who the girl in the picture was? Even we don't know that, and we're family!"

"We think," Xena said, "that it wasn't a girl at all. We think it was a boy, one of Nigel Batheson's sons, dressed up to look like a girl!"

Xena waited for their reaction. Would they laugh at them? Have them thrown out of the museum?

For a moment there was silence. Then the man with the mustache said, "What a fascinating theory! Which son do you think it was?" he asked Xander.

"We're not sure," Xander answered. "We don't know much about Nigel's children except that they went to boarding school and one had smallpox and another liked toads."

"Maybe you could help," Xena said. "Do you know which one might have been about eight years old when Nigel painted the portrait?"

The tall Batheson turned to Mrs. Emerson. "Here, Emily, you always have a little of everything in that bag of yours. Could you find a bit of paper and something to write with? Let's see what we can remember."

Mrs. Emerson dug in her purse and produced an envelope and the stub of a pencil. One of the Batheson men cleared a space on a small table that was littered with paper napkins and empty glasses, and the adults all put their heads together. Xena and Xander stood on tiptoe peering over their shoulders.

The little snippets of conversation they heard just tantalized them more. "Abner was born when, Jack?" and "But I thought their cousin Frank was older than Cedric." Just when they thought they would burst with curiosity, the adults moved aside a little and let them see what they had been working on.

It was a family tree. Birth years of most of the relatives had been penciled in. There were no daughters, no female cousins, not even an aunt who would have been a young girl when the painting was done.

Xander studied the paper carefully. "So if *Girl in a Purple Hat* was painted in 1902 and Abner was born in 1885, he'd be too old to be the model."

"Cedric was born in 1890," Xena remarked. "That would make him twelve. That's a little too old, even if he looked young for his age. And, anyway, he had smallpox scars on his face by then."

"But Robert," Xander went on. "He was born in 1894."

"That would have made him eight when the painting was made!" Xena exclaimed. "That's about the age of the model in the painting. It could be him!"

"That is so clever of you, children," the man with the mustache said. "And just think of all the art historians who haven't been able to figure this out."

Blushing but pleased, Xena pocketed the envelope with the Batheson family tree on it. Then they said good-bye to the Bathesons and left the room.

"So where do we go from here?" Xena asked. "How does knowing who modeled for *Girl in a Purple Hat* help us figure out who stole it?"

Xander didn't have a response for that. He took his coat from the hook where he had hung it on his way in. When he put it on, the picture of him in his daisy costume fell out of a pocket.

"Hey!" Xena cried. "My picture!"

Xander quickly swiped it off the floor. "It's *my* picture now," he said. "I told you. You're not getting it back. I don't trust you not to show it again."

"So you're going to carry it with you everywhere?" Xena asked. "Or will you tear it up?"

"Maybe," Xander replied, though he knew that he wouldn't. There was something—well, something weird about tearing up his own picture. But as soon as he got back to their apartment, he'd hide it deep under his mattress.

And that's exactly what he did. Then, with his arm shoved halfway underneath his mattress, he realized something about the mystery.

Xena didn't think the identity of Batheson's model in *Girl in a Purple Hat* mattered. But it did matter . . . it was the key to solving the whole case!

CHAPTER 15

I solved the case! I solved the case!" Xander raced into his sister's bedroom down the hall.

Xena was sitting on her bed, the casebook open on her lap. "Slow down," she said. "What are you talking about, Xander?"

Xander took a big gulp of air. "I figured out who took the painting," he said. "It was Robert. It had to be."

"How did you get to that?" Xena asked.

"Don't you see?" Xander asked eagerly. "Even though that picture of me is totally embarrassing, I couldn't bear to tear it up. So I decided to hide it instead. I bet that's what happened to the painting!"

Understanding was dawning in Xena's eyes. "So maybe Robert did the same thing!"

"He was the youngest and his big brothers probably teased him," Xander went on. "I'll bet his brothers made fun of him about it for years!

I mean, what brother wouldn't?" Then his face fell as he thought of something. "But then the house got bombed. I bet the painting was destroyed."

"Maybe not," Xena said slowly. "Robert wasn't home for most of the year, right? He went away to school."

"Right," Xander said. "Maybe he took it to school with him."

"Who says he didn't take it back home too?" Xena asked.

"He might have," Xander admitted. "But maybe nobody else knew he took the painting to school, and he figured no one would ever find it, so he just left it there. What if after all these years it's still there?"

"We have to find out where Robert went to boarding school." Xena leaped up and began to pace around the room. "What about the letters in the library?" She stopped. "Oh, *darn*!"

"What?" Xander asked.

"The library's closed over the weekend," she said. "We can't wait until Monday! We're almost there!"

"It doesn't matter," Xander said. "The name of Robert's school isn't mentioned in the letters."

"How do you know that?" Xena asked.

"Uh, hello?" Xander tapped a finger on his head. "Photographic memory, remember?"

Xena picked up the casebook and flipped through it. "The answer has got to be in here somewhere." She pored through Sherlock Holmes's notes for about the millionth time.

"Taynesbury." With that note, Sherlock had led them to where Nigel and his family had lived. "Abner, Cedric, Robert." That was the list of the artist's sons that the great detective had made. Then the note, "Model?" Sherlock had wondered who the model was too. And finally there was that doodle of a dragon.

"I just know I've seen that someplace," Xander said, pointing to the drawing. "But where?"

"Huh!" said Xena. "Why don't you use that famous photographic memory of yours?"

"All that tells me is that I've seen it," he pointed out. "It doesn't tell me *where*. And I bet it's important to the case. Sherlock doesn't seem like the type to write all of these important notes and then mess up the page with a doodle."

Xena stared at it. "It's not a very good picture either," she said. "Where are its legs, and how could fire come from it if the thing is twisted into a circle and has its own tail shoved in its mouth?"

Taynesbury

4 March 1907
Nigel Batheson~Girl
in a Purple Hat
Noticed missing Thursday last.

in London a...
g else missing from...
go

...mily
...Marguerite
Abr...
Cedru...
Robert

who
...irl?

e o...

Perhaps Ghastly children had birthday celebration on the 10th.
Ghastly children ... ...sible creatures):

Note:
Manor house vacant
until Xmas

Purple hat borrowed fro...
neighbor's daughter~but
she was not subject
of painting.

Xander thought about it some more. "Maybe it's *not* a dragon," he said.

"I know!" Xena said. She ran out to the living room and came back holding a magnifying glass. Enlarged, the drawing wasn't much clearer. They could see, though, that what had looked like one dragon with its tail in its mouth was actually two separate creatures.

Xena sat back and said, "Sherlock Holmes was a great detective, but he was not a great artist."

But why does the picture feel so familiar? Xander wondered. He closed his eyes, willing the answer to come to him. And then, a vision of two scaly blue and yellow creatures surged into his brain. Two ferocious sea serpents twisted in battle.

And there was something else. A shield. Then a green background. It was a jersey. On a kid who was playing soccer.

Knuckers.

"Xander?" Xena put a hand on his shoulder. "What is it? What's the matter?"

Xander turned to his sister, and his dark blue eyes met her brown eyes. "I think I know what Sherlock Holmes was trying to draw," he said. "It wasn't a dragon at all—it was two knuckers!"

Xena traced the sketch with a finger. "You're right! It's all falling into place. Sherlock must have known that the mascot for Robert Batheson's school was a knucker. That's why he drew this."

Xander nodded. "And I bet he would have checked out the school next if he hadn't been called away on another case."

"The Giraffes played the Knuckers in a scrimmage," Xena said. "That means the school can't be too far away. We have to go there!"

The next day Xena and Xander headed out with bus fare, directions, and a plan. They would go to Worthington, Robert Batheson's old boarding school and the home of the Knuckers, to search for the painting. Xander scribbled a note to their mother, saying that they were taking a bus to the school that their school was playing in soccer.

"I didn't say we were going to a game," he told Xena when she looked doubtful. "It's all true."

"I don't know," Xena said, and then she shrugged. "Well, they know that we're pretty good at riding the bus and tube systems by now, so they shouldn't worry. And I thought of something else." She let herself into their mother's study and pulled out the latest box of gadgets from the testing company. She picked out a few and showed them to Xander.

"Good idea," he said as she shoved some of them into a backpack. You never knew what would come in handy.

The trip took longer than they thought, since they had to ride the Tube to the end of the line and then catch a bus that seemed to stop at every street corner. It was agonizing.

Pretty soon the houses started getting more and more widely spaced, and they saw yards and dogs and swing sets. Xena chewed her knuckle in exasperation. Would they never get there?

The trees were big and most had lost their leaves. The sky was growing dark, even though it was still early.

"Storm coming," Xander said. He looked out the bus window as Xena consulted the directions to see how much farther they had to go.

Finally Xena said, "Just another few blocks," and the next time the bus creaked to a halt they climbed off.

WORTHINGTON SCHOOL FOR BOYS read a tarnished metal plaque on the gate of a wrought-iron fence right next to the bus stop. They looked up at the school. It was a grim old stone place with sooty walls.

"Check it out," Xena said, pointing at the

round emblem on the metal plaque. Even through the tarnish the twisted shape of the knuckers, curled around on themselves, was just like the drawing in the casebook.

"It looks like the school's been here forever," Xander said.

"A hundred years, at least," Xena said as she pushed open the gate. "Come on. Let's see if we can find the dorm."

They were farther away from the city than they had realized from the printed directions. Leaves swirled around their feet, carrying the spicy-sweet scent of autumn to their nostrils. A dog barked in the distance, and the wind picked up. Xander felt the back of his neck prickle.

"Hey, wait!" he called and trotted to catch up to Xena.

A bell rang as some students hurried past them with books under their arms. A beefy boy squinted at Xander. Another boy said, "We're going to be late for study group if you don't hurry," and the first boy turned and followed the others through a tall wooden door.

Then Xena and Xander were alone again. "Who was that?" Xena asked. "He acted as though he recognized you."

"He was that jerk at the soccer game," Xander

said. "The one who stole the ball from me."

"Huh," Xena said. She opened the door the boys had gone through and stepped inside, followed closely by Xander.

But the corridor was lined with classrooms, not bedrooms, and the smell of chalkboards told them that they were in the wrong place. Any minute someone could come by and accuse them of trespassing. Which was exactly what they were doing.

"There's got to be some kind of a dorm someplace," Xena said. "But we can't just stumble around until we find it."

One of the doors facing them had a sign on it saying OFFICE. Xena paused in front of it. "Xander, in those letters, did Robert's mother say what his room number was?" she asked.

"No," he said.

"Great," Xena muttered. "We'll just have to ask someone."

She knocked on the office door. No answer. She knocked louder. Still nothing. She and Xander looked at each other. He shrugged. What else can we do? his expression said. So she pushed the door open.

At first it looked like no one was there. And then they saw a body.

CHAPTER 16

It was a man's body, right in front of them. They couldn't see his face because he was leaning back in a big chair, his feet on a desk, his head dangling down at an unnatural angle.

Xander grabbed Xena's hand. "Is he dead?" he whispered hoarsely.

"I don't know," Xena answered, her throat tight, and just at that moment a loud sound made them jump.

It was a snore, and it came from the man in the chair. Xander dropped Xena's hand and tried to pretend that he hadn't touched her.

Xena stepped forward. "Sir?" she said. A grunt. She took a deep breath, then reached out and shook his shoulder.

He opened one eye. "Yes?" he asked. Then he sat up. "You're not students here," he said suspiciously.

"Bingo," Xena said.

"What?"

"Nothing," Xander said. He didn't want Xena's sarcasm to get them kicked out. He turned his most winning smile on the man, who appeared to be a custodian, and told him the story that he and Xena had come up with on the bus ride, that their grandfather had been a student there. Xena couldn't tell whether the man was won over by Xander's charm or whether he just wanted him to shut up and let him go back to sleep, because he finally said, "Just what is it you kids want?"

"We just want to see his room," Xander said.

"So go see it," the man said.

"But we don't know the room number," Xena said.

"Can't help you there," the man said, settling back down. "Records were destroyed in a fire."

"Where are the dorms?" Xander asked.

"Go out the main door, turn left, next building you see."

"Thanks," Xena said and they left.

The low two-story brick building that faced them had to be the dormitory. Curtains hung in the windows, and bikes stood in a rack by the door.

"Now what?" Xander asked.

"I think I can figure it out," Xena said. "Come on."

The long corridor inside was a little more cheery than the one in the first building. A worn carpet lay on the floor, and on the doors hung whiteboards with felt pens dangling on strings. "Gone home for weekend," read one, and "Sign up for crew practice" was on another.

Xena followed her brother, wandering around long passages and up, then down, narrow staircases. A boy wearing a bathrobe came out of a room and looked at them curiously, but most of the students seemed to be out.

"I've been thinking about those letters," Xena said. "In one, Robert mentioned that he had to get up so early that while he was getting dressed he could watch the sun rise from his window."

"The sun rises in the east and sets in the west," Xander said, getting it now. "So his room must be on the east side of the house. *This* side," he said, pointing. "Anything else?"

Xena nodded, concentrating. "The headmaster said Robert put a toad in the bed of the boy upstairs from him—remember? So his room had to be on the first floor. There are only two floors, and if he was on the second floor, there wouldn't be a boy above him." The words were tumbling out of her now. "He also said that the sound of running water in the pipes reminded him of the brook at home."

They stood in front of a door next to the bathroom. "This has to be it," Xena decided. "The bathroom's at the end of the hall, so this is the only room right next to the pipes. East side, first floor."

Xander knocked. No answer. Xena knocked harder, and the door swung open. They looked at each other, gathered their nerve, and entered.

CHAPTER 17

Xena flicked on a light. It looked like an ordinary bedroom, with a single bed, a desk piled with books and a lamp, a chest of drawers, and against the wall, a tall wardrobe with double doors.

Xander pulled a bandanna from his pocket and blew his nose. The place smelled like it hadn't been dusted in a century.

Xena opened the wardrobe door and looked in, half expecting to see *Girl in a Purple Hat* frowning at her from the top shelf.

"No painting," she said. "No Narnia either," she added.

She turned to see Xander shoving himself underneath the mattress on the bed. He pulled back, his brown curls jutting out in every direction. "Nothing," he said, and Xena laughed as he sneezed. "Hey, it was worth a shot," he said. "But the only thing under there is a collection of old comic books." He blew his nose again.

"This is ridiculous," Xena said. "The painting has been hidden for more than a hundred years. It wouldn't be anywhere out in the open." She surveyed the room, her hands on her hips. On the desk was a small family photo. No paintings.

"Maybe it's behind a wall," she mused. "That's the only way it could have stayed hidden this long."

Xander's eyes turned to the wood paneling. "I bet it wouldn't be hard to pry one of those pieces of wood out and slide something like a painting behind it."

But Xena was rummaging around in the backpack. "Aha!" she said, pulling out a small object enclosed in shrink-wrap.

"What's that?" Xander asked as she worked the plastic off.

"Remember when Dad was hanging that wall cabinet in the dining room back home?" she asked. "He said it was so heavy that screws would pull out of the plaster, so he had to find those pieces of wood in the wall, those supports—what do you call them?"

"Studs," Xander said and kicked the wall.

"Cut that out," Xena said. "Someone will hear you. Anyway, he knocked with his knuckles so he could hear where they were but he couldn't tell so he got a little machine that could tell where the supports were. Well, ta-da!" She held up the object, now freed from its wrapping. "We have one! This is one of the gadgets from Mom's company. It's like a stud-finder, but instead it locates metal. It's supposed to be extremely sensitive."

"So?"

Honestly, sometimes Xander could be so dense!

"Don't you see? The only place left to look is behind a wall, and we can't just go and tear down the whole thing."

"Sister dear," Xander said with deep sarcasm in his voice. "I think you've forgotten something. This is a painting we're looking for, not a nail. Paint. Wood. No metal."

"Brother dear," Xena answered, her tone matching his. "Think about the paintings we saw at the gallery. Remember the frames, the ones you thought were so cool? Gold frames. Hung with thick metal wires. Metal all *over* them."

Maybe she was right. He didn't know if a metal detector could find gold, but those wires were the kind of thing they could locate.

"Well, okay. But how does that help?" Xander asked. "We can't tear the room up. That would be vandalism."

"I know," Xena said. "But if it's behind the wall and we find out exactly where it is, we can take off just one panel. I'm sure that would be okay."

"No way," Xander said, but it was too late. Xena was holding the stud-finder up to the wall. "Oh, *shoot*!" she said, and the look of frustration on her face would have made Xander laugh if he hadn't been so worried about getting caught.

"What is it?"

"I didn't know it needed batteries!"

Silently, Xander opened his own backpack and pulled out his portable CD player.

Xena snatched it and pried open the battery case. "You're not supposed to have that at school," she said.

"I know." Xander was watching her insert the batteries into the stud-finder. "I forgot I had it. If Dad would just let me download tunes off the Internet, I'd have a—"

Xena wasn't listening. She tossed the instructions to Xander. "Hurry up," she instructed. "Get that speed-reading thing going in your brain and tell me what to do."

"Turn it on first," he said.

"Duh," she answered.

"Well, you were the one who forgot the batteries," he said reasonably. "How would I know you'd remember to turn it on?"

"Okay, okay. What do I do next?"

Following his instructions, she moved the small plastic box over the wall. At one point the needle swung over to the right.

"Metal," she muttered.

"But it might be one of those stud things," he pointed out.

She moved it again, and the needle dropped back down to the left, to zero. At regular intervals—they didn't have a ruler so they couldn't tell exactly how far it was—the needle would swing over. It got to be predictable: every eighteen inches or so they'd find what had to be another stud.

Then, suddenly, less than six inches after the last one, the needle swung over and stayed on the right as though glued there. Xena moved the little box slowly and still the needle clung stubbornly to the red part of the scale.

Their eyes met. "There's something in there," Xena said slowly. "Something made of metal, and long, like a wire or a frame, not a nail."

CHAPTER 18

Now what? How could they pry off a strip of wood paneling without damaging the wall? Come to think of it, how could they pry it off at all? Xena tried to grasp the edge of the wood.

"Can you get a grip on it?" Xander was breathing on the back of her neck.

"Quit it," she said, shrugging him away. She held up her hands. "Too bad I keep my nails short." She shook her head. "If I had long nails like some of the girls at school I could pry it up enough to get a grip."

"What if the person whose room this is comes back?" Xander asked.

"That's a risk we have to take," Xena said, but she didn't feel as confident as she sounded. What were the penalties for breaking and entering anyway? And did they allow you a phone call if you were arrested in England, like they did in the States? She looked at the wood panel again and spat on her hands. Maybe with a little friction—

But before she could try again, Xander tugged at her arm.

"Look!" he said, pointing out the window.

Xena glanced out and groaned. Boys were streaming across the courtyard toward the dorm.

"We'll just tell them about the painting," Xander said. "We'll tell them—"

"Forget it!" Xena said. "They'd never believe us. They're not about to tear up a wall just because two American kids say that there's a famous painting behind it. Would *you* believe that story?"

"Yes," Xander said stubbornly, but he didn't mean it. He knew it sounded nuts. And worse, now he heard voices echoing in the corridor.

"I tell you, I saw someone in there," said a boy, adding, "sir."

"Nonsense," came the deeper voice of a man. "Who would break into your room?"

"I don't know," said the boy. "But I saw—"

"Quick," Xena said under her breath. "No time to lose." In one swift motion, she shoved her brother under the bed, then slid herself under as well. They were in the middle of what looked like an entire family of dust bunnies, but at least they were invisible to anyone standing up—she hoped. And she hoped that Xander's allergies wouldn't betray them with a sneeze.

They tried to quiet their breathing as the door opened. Xander's heart was pounding so loudly he was sure that the whole of England could hear it. He swallowed.

"See, nobody here," the man's voice said.

"But I *know* I saw someone," the boy answered. "The light was on and the curtains were open . . ."

Oh, shoot, Xena thought. Why didn't we think to close the curtains? She would have slapped her own forehead for stupidity if she hadn't been worried about the noise.

"Is anything missing?" the man asked. There was a pause.

"No," the boy finally said. "I don't think so. But this picture is moved." A small scraping sound must mean that he was lining the photographs up on his desk again.

"Would a thief be interested in your family photos?" the man asked, after a pause. It sounded as if he was trying hard to be reasonable.

"No, sir," the boy mumbled.

"Well, then, let's just go on," the man said.

"I'm sure you have some work to do in preparation for the exam on Monday, don't you?"

"Yes, sir," the boy said.

Xander allowed himself to relax a little.

The door opened again, and the man's heavier footsteps sounded in the hallway. Xena and Xander looked at each other. What if the boy stayed here to do his studying? They heard rustling sounds. Xena longed to peek out from under the bed, but why risk getting caught when they were so close?

"Coming, Fraser?" the man called from outside the door.

"Just gathering my papers, sir," the boy called.

A pause. What could he be doing? Then, "What's this?" came the boy's voice, higher-pitched than before.

"What's what?" The man seemed at the edge of his patience.

"This, sir." There was no mistaking his excitement. "I found this on the floor. It's not mine. I've never seen it before. What is it?"

This time it was Xander who almost slapped himself on the forehead. The stud-finder! They had left it right in plain view!

Footsteps again. Xander couldn't resist a

quick peek. He saw a youngish-looking man with blond hair. He was standing with—oh no, it was the boy who had acted as if he recognized Xander. The man took the stud-finder from the boy's hand and turned it over slowly.

"Why, it's a—"

"Ah-choo!" Xena exploded next to him.

CHAPTER 19

For a moment all anyone could do was stare. Underneath the bed, Xander stared at Xena. *She* was the one who sneezed? Xena stared at the man who was now on his hands and knees staring at them, and the boy stared at everybody.

The man stepped back and Xena and Xander scrambled out. They stood together, not knowing where to look.

"Now," said the man. "Who are you? Why are you hiding under this bed?"

But before either one of them could say anything, the boy broke in. "I know you!" He was pointing at Xander, who looked back at him and winced.

"I know you too," he said. "You're the guy who stole the ball from me at the soccer game."

The boy snorted, a grin on his face. "You Yanks just don't know how to play footer," he said.

"We do too!" Xander said hotly and would

have gone on, except that the man, standing with his hands on his hips, interrupted them.

"Let's continue this discussion of sport superiority another time," he said. "I'm Mr. Nolan, the art master. You'd better have a good excuse for being in Fraser's room."

Xena took a deep breath. "Well, you see, it's like this," she began. "We're detectives, and we're direct descendants of Sherlock Holmes." She stopped, knowing she must sound ridiculous.

"Go on," Mr. Nolan said, and Xander thought he saw the corner of the man's mouth twitch as though he was trying not to smile.

So Xena told him the whole story, interrupted by Xander when he felt the need to add a detail.

The boy made little disbelieving noises, but Mr. Nolan hushed him and turned his attention back to their story.

Finally Xena stopped talking and once again silence fell.

"Please help us," she went on after a moment. "We don't have any more clues. If *Girl in a Purple Hat* isn't here, we'll have to give up."

"Brilliant!" the art teacher finally said. "It's strange, but it makes sense. I've always wondered what happened to that painting." And he broke into a broad grin.

"So we can take off a panel?" Xander asked eagerly.

"Not so fast." Mr. Nolan held up a hand. "Fraser," he said, turning to the boy, "please go to the head's office and ask him to come here."

"Why me?" the boy asked, his face sulky. "Why not send one of them?"

"What?" said Mr. Nolan with a laugh. "And give these dangerous criminals a chance to escape? I think not. No, you go."

A few minutes later they heard voices in the corridor.

"In here, sir," Fraser said as he opened the door. In came a tall man with steel gray hair.

"Well, Nolan?" he said as he rubbed his hands together. "Fraser's been telling me quite a story. What about it?"

The art teacher told the headmaster an abbreviated version of Xena's tale. "I suppose it could have happened that way," the headmaster said, and he turned to Xena. "Where do you think it might be hidden?"

Xena pointed silently and the headmaster gave the wall a few taps.

"It *does* sound as if something could be rattling around in there." He patted his robe as though feeling for something in the pockets of his clothes underneath it. "Nolan?" he said. "Got a penknife, anything of that sort?"

The art teacher made a regretful noise. "Sorry, sir," he said.

"Fraser?"

The boy opened a desk drawer and pulled out a multibladed pocketknife.

"Thanks," said the headmaster. "And I'll be taking this with me when we're through. You know you're not allowed knives in school."

The boy turned to Xena and Xander and shot them a venomous look.

Meanwhile the headmaster had opened the longest blade and was running his fingers down the edge of the board in question. "Mind you, it's probably just a pipe or some ductwork in there," he cautioned as he worked the blade into the crack.

The board popped out. It left a hole that ran from the floor to the ceiling, but it was no more than six inches wide. "Not even nailed down," he said. "Interesting!" He slid his hand and wrist into the opening, grunting a little as he tried to reach behind the panel. "Can't reach in far enough," he said. "The opening's too small."

"Let's take out another piece!" Xander blurted.

"No," said the headmaster. "We don't want a

large repair bill for what might turn out to be a wild goose chase."

"Care to give it a try?" the art teacher asked Xander. Xander stepped forward. But although his arm could fit into the opening, it wasn't long enough to reach very far. He looked at his sister.

"Xena?"

She nodded. Xander and the headmaster stood back.

Xena rolled her sleeve up to her shoulder and flexed her fingers a few times. Then she closed her eyes, took a deep breath, and reached inside.

CHAPTER 20

At first—nothing. Xena stretched her fingers and nearly dislocated her shoulder twisting deeper into the hole.

"Anything?" Xander's voice was hoarse with tension.

"Not yet," she said, but just then her fingers grazed the cold, hard edge of something. "Got it!" she said.

"Got what?" Xander asked.

"Something hard," she said. "And I think I can hook a finger around this wire." Everyone watched in silence as she wriggled and strained. Then slowly, gently, she pulled.

With surprising ease, the thing moved. She pulled again. Whatever it was slid along the wall, nearer and nearer.

"Careful!" The art teacher was nearly dancing up and down in excitement. "Don't damage it! Here, let me take out another board." This time the headmaster didn't object as Mr. Nolan popped off a second piece of the paneling with the knife.

Xena reached in again, and as the others leaned forward, holding their breath, her arm moved, and then her hand emerged. It grasped a gold-colored frame, and in the frame was . . .

Girl in a Purple Hat.

Time seemed to stand still as they gazed at it. Even Fraser was speechless.

No wonder the paper had said that the copies hadn't done justice to the original. The expression on the face had looked bratty in the newspaper and even in the copies that the artist had been making. Here, the face was sulky, to be sure, but Batheson had painted his subject with such humor and affection that you could tell that in just a moment he could tease her—or him—into smiling. The colors in the background were softer than in the copies they'd seen, which made the brilliant green of the model's eyes stand out even more.

"It's like he's looking right at you," Xander whispered.

"Or glaring at you," Xena replied. "Robert must have been *really* mad. Not only because his dad made him pose like that, but because he knew people would see him wearing a dress."

Xander nodded. "Tell me about it."

The next hour was full of confusion. The headmaster called their parents and then called a news organization. Teachers and students crowded the little room and spilled out into the hall, all of them asking questions and exclaiming over the painting, which Mr. Nolan was holding as though it were made of glass.

Their taxi ride home was much quicker than the bus trip out. Still, it was enough time for the story of their discovery to spread. When they walked in the door of their flat, they heard the news of the amazing Batheson find at the Worthington School for Boys coming from the TV.

The next day was almost as unbelievable as the find itself. Right after breakfast, the phone rang. It was Andrew.

"Good job," he said to Xena. "Congratulations. You two are all right." Xena knew that coming from Andrew this was high praise, and she felt herself blushing.

"Thanks," she said.

There was a pause and then Andrew said gruffly, "Sorry about the way I treated you at the beginning. Aunt Mary reminded me that Watson was Holmes's best friend and he'd be unhappy if we didn't get along. Pax?"

"Huh?" Xena asked, and Andrew burst out into the first real laugh she had heard from him.

"It means 'peace' in Latin," he explained. "It's kind of old-fashioned, but it's a way to ask if we can stop quarreling." He sounded embarrassed and went on before she could answer. "And I'm supposed to ask you and your parents to a special meeting of the Society for the Preservation of Famous Detectives this evening. But not in the usual place. This time it will be at the Victoria and Albert."

"The coolest museum in London!" she exclaimed. "That's where the Batheson exhibit is."

"Got it in one," Andrew replied, and then he said good-bye.

After a quick supper, the whole family went down to the Tube station. They got out of the train at the South Kensington stop and climbed up onto the sidewalk. The huge red-and-white museum loomed over them.

"This *is* a cool building," Xander said as they walked up the staircase. A uniformed guard opened the door with a flourish. Andrew was waiting just inside.

"Where are we going?" Xena asked him.

"This way," Andrew answered.

"Big help," Xena said, but they followed him

down the wide corridor of medieval art, through the garden, and straight ahead to a room with stained-glass windows and bright tiles.

"In here!" trilled a familiar voice.

"Aunt Mary?" Xander asked.

"In the flesh!"

Andrew pushed open a door, and there were the members of the SPFD. All of them wore huge smiles.

"Isn't this lovely?" Aunt Mary said. "All of Batheson's paintings are together here for one more day, before they go on tour . . . *including* the lost painting that you two found!"

"Wow!" Their mom sounded impressed. "The painting you found just *makes* the show!"

Abner at the Fair hung on the wall to Aunt Mary's left, and *Cedric Flying a Kite* was to her right. Xena and Xander couldn't see the other paintings through the crowd.

Aunt Mary opened her arms. "I knew you were detectives at heart," she said and sniffled as she hugged them.

"I've always thought they showed great aptitude," their father said. He was beaming.

"We're extremely proud," their mother added.

"You two have exceeded our expectations,"

said Mr. Brown, and from all around them came murmurs of "Congratulations!" and "Well done!" Then everyone sang "For they are jolly good fellows!" while Xena and Xander stood awkwardly in the center of the room, not knowing where to look or what to do with their hands.

That problem was taken care of as soon as the song was over. A beaming man with messy brown hair came in carrying a large package wrapped in brown paper.

"I'm Mr. Fontaine," he said. "Louis Fontaine, the curator of the Victoria and Albert Museum, and I have a small gift to express the appreciation of this museum and this country. You have restored a masterpiece to us that we thought was lost."

Xander grinned as he remembered Xena shoving him under the bed in Fraser's room.

"We are forever grateful," Mr. Fontaine went on, "and we hope you will accept this gift with our sincere thanks."

Xander took the package. "Thank you," he said. "Should we open it now?"

"Please," said Mr. Fontaine, and stood back as they untied the string and then unwound the layers of brown paper.

What on earth? All they could do was blink.

"You've given us—" Xander started, but he couldn't finish. *Girl in a Purple Hat* was for them?

Then Xena laughed. "Look at her eyes," she said, and with a rush of relief and a little disappointment, Xander saw that they were brown, not the startling green of the original.

"Oh, this is one of the copies that the artist was making!" he exclaimed.

Mr. Fontaine nodded. "It will look good hanging in your sitting room, don't you think?"

"It will look *awesome*," Xena said. Xander nodded in agreement. Behind them, the room erupted in cheers.

Xena grinned at Xander and he grinned back. He knew what she was thinking. And he was thinking the same thing.

They were proud that they had found the missing painting and made so many people happy—but that wasn't the best part of the adventure.

The best part was that they hadn't failed their ancestor, the greatest detective who had ever lived. Sherlock Holmes, they both knew, would have been proud.